I0630874

THE DARK OF MIDNIGHT & OTHER STORIES

STEPHEN MERTZ

WOLFPACK
PUBLISHING
— EST 2013 —

The Dark of Midnight & Other Stories is a work of fiction. Any references to historical events, real people or real places are used fictitiously. Other names, characters, places and events are products of the author's imagination, and any resemblance to actual events, places or persons, living or dead, is entirely coincidental.

Copyright © 2018 by Stephen Mertz
All rights reserved.

Published in the United States by Wolfpack Publishing

Wolfpack Publishing
6032 Wheat Penny Avenue
Las Vegas, NV 89122

wolfpackpublishing.com

Library of Congress Control Number: 2018951500

Paperback ISBN: 978-1-64119-281-1
eBook ISBN: 978-1-64119-264-4

PRAISE FOR STEPHEN MERTZ

"One of my favorite writers ... a born storyteller ... Enjoy!"

--Max Allan Collins, NYT Bestselling author of *Road to Perdition* and the *Quarry* series.

"One of the best adventure writers of our time!"

--NYT Bestselling writer James Reasoner

"Stephen Mertz just keeps on getting better, each novel more dazzling in story and style!"

--Ed Gorman

THE DARK OF MIDNIGHT & OTHER STORIES

I

THE LIZARD MEN OF BLOOD RIVER: A SPEED MCCOY NOVELETTE

INTRODUCTION

All writers write pastiche in the beginning.

At an early age, usually, the creative spark is ignited when we read Steinbeck or Spillane or Burroughs (either one), and we want to grow up to write just like 'em. Later, a professional writer's early career generally involves writing fiction to formula, honing the craft in low rent genre markets. The third step, for writers of ambition and worth, is to graduate to developing your own voice, refining your own formulae.

Yet, one should never forget one's raisin'.

Just for fun, then, here's a nod to a personal favorite old pulp writer whose identity will become apparent in due course. The author of hundreds of pulp magazine novels and stories (many of them highly regarded), he revealed in 1936 that every piece of fiction he'd ever published adhered to a Master Plot Formula of his own devising.

When I was invited to contribute a pulp story

pastiche for this collection, I could not resist referring and adhering to that old master formula, just to see how it would work for the writer I have become.

The guy claimed that 780 people subsequently wrote him to say that they'd tried his formula and sold their story. A ridiculous number, I know, but hey, he was a paid teller of tales. But if that claim is valid, the story you are about to read notches the number up to 781.

BLOOD RIVER

The sound of jungle drums, muted but incessant, wafted in through the open windows of the Zeppelin's promenade deck. Beyond the windows, the tropical sunset was an angry vermilion, mirrored by the river passing 650-feet below, making its surging waters appear as a red, pulsating river of blood.

Sonya Whittaker, standing next to Speed McCoy, gazed out upon the emerald carpet of darkening green and sighed wistfully.

"Those drums. Beautiful, is it not, Mr. McCoy? Like a symphony composed of this breathtaking land itself?"

She was twenty years old, endowed with the sharp features of her father's Celtic genes and the mane of midnight black hair and dusky, almond-eyed beauty of her deceased mother's Brazilian heritage combined with some exotic, perhaps forgotten Asian race.

Speed said, "Those are war drums. These tribes of

the Mato Grosso are the most savage in the whole of South America. Not one of them has yet moved out of the Stone Age. The jungle is crawling with them, right below us. Headhunters and cannibals. They could be discussing what tasty meals we'll make."

"Remnants of an ancient civilization hiding among the silent trees. I find it enthralling."

"Sure, if you like dirty rivers and swamps full of poison snakes. Ever seen a Giant Anaconda, or what it can do to a man?"

Sonya lapsed into reverie without responding.

Speed McCoy was a tall man, well-muscled, ruggedly built. He wore a cartridge belt with a .44 revolver holstered low on his right hip. He shifted his attention to the men and women at the far end of the promenade deck, which was attached to the airship's cabin like a balcony.

Sonya's father, the Colonel, was holding court. Like his guests, Colonel Whittaker wore starched khaki. He was brusque and hearty. A bristly white mustache riding above a square jaw was his most prominent feature. He wore a pith helmet.

"AND SO YOU SEE, MY FRIENDS," he was saying, "there is sufficient reason to believe that a highly advanced ancient civilization did indeed once inhabit this region. My lovely daughter," he nodded proudly in Sonya's direction, "who serves as my research assistant whenever she's on break from her studies at the university, will attest to the diligence and breadth of my research. The answers to the enigmas of prehistoric civilization will be found when their ancient cities are located and opened to scientific research."

There was an enthusiastic murmur from his sycophants.

This excursion, financed by the Colonel, who had invited along a select group of his high society friends, was taking them deep into uncharted country. They thought it was an adventure. They thought it was fun. They thought they were safe.

Speed thought they were nuts. But he'd been flat broke and so had taken on this job as a watchdog for the Five Star Line, which considered his presence an adequate measure in overseeing their interests in leasing the luxury dirigible to the Colonel.

THEY HAD LIFTED off from Rio de Janeiro's Campo de Affonso Army Air Field. The dirigible's long gray shadow blotted out the sun as it passed over the beaches of Copacabana and Ipanema. The pilot had circled Corcovado Mountain with the statue of Christ on top, then the Zeppelin's cigar-shaped shadow flew over the white salt flats of Cabo Frio, past fishing fleets with their reeling flocks of seagulls, following the coastline north, diverting inland on the third day only when they reached the mouth of the Amazon.

One of the Colonel's sycophants was saying, "Wouldn't it be a jolly good show to find this lost city from the air? Fascinating to consider that a country this hostile could host any such large-scale settlement."

A slim, dapper Brazilian of slight build stood beside the Colonel. Juan Callas was the only one present not wearing khaki. He wore a formal frock coat. It was said that Callas had first whetted the Colonel's appetite for this expedition months earlier with theories and alleged evidence of ancient cultures in the region.

Callas said, "Eminent paleontologists consider this to be the oldest continent on Earth; perhaps, the most ancient civilization of mankind. Western knowledge has tended to treat this rainforest as one big homogeneous jungle, a laboratory for Stone Age primitives frozen at the dawn of time." He spoke in a vaguely sibilant monotone that implied a dismissal of any skepticism. "Due in large part to the generosity of Colonel Whittaker and," he bowed gallantly in Sonya's direct, "his lovely daughter, we shall prove that a superior prehistoric race once ruled this land with sorcery at the dawn of time."

"ASCENDED MASTERS OF WISDOM," said the Colonel, savoring the phrase. "Think of it. A lost city, a tribe with civilization more advanced than our own, choosing to remain hidden in this hostile land; from another dimension, perhaps, with the intention of helping our planet shape its destiny. Earth Guardians"

THIS, apparently, was the sort of talk that transpired at the hoity-toity soirées of these idle rich.

The City of Rio was cruising at a leisurely 50 mph, heading upriver over the moist broadleaf rainforest of the upper Xingu region of the southern Amazon; seven million square kilometers of forbidding, impenetrable wilderness.

A short time later, with the conversation prattling on, Callas nonchalantly left the Colonel's side. He eased unobtrusively toward a doorway.

Speed nodded politely to Sonya and followed. There was something about the dapper little man that got under Speed's skin. He sensed something sinister about the fellow. He passed through the doorway and stiff-legged across the red-flowered carpet covered floor of the comfortable lounge that served as a dining room for meals. The velvet curtains were drawn. The dirigible's propellers and outside motors were barely audible. There was no sign of Juan Callas.

IN A SMALL ANTEROOM just outside of the lounge, a hall in one direction led to the staterooms. The dirigible's passenger accommodations resembled a first-class railroad coach, complete with the finest amenities. The control, chart and radio rooms at the front of the gondola were in the opposite direction. Skeleton-like stairs led up into the body of the ship.

Speed ascended the stairs two at a time, pursuing the only route Callas could have taken in the short time available to him. He emerged from the top to become engulfed by the cavernous enormity of the inside of the Zeppelin. He was on the narrow keel catwalk that rigidly extended along the center length of this monstrosity of alloy and fabric, an eerie, cavernous half-darkness poorly illuminated with the artificial twilight of evenly but distantly spaced electric bulbs.

There was, however, enough illumination to discern Juan Callas, crouching furtively near the stern where a latitudinal catwalk joined a master ring girder that reached up and outward around the ship. The little man was a hunched shadow at the base of one of the *Rio's* massive hydrogen cell balloonets.

"*Callas!* What are you doing up there?" Speed's sharp query echoed through the cavernous bowels of the airship.

Callas jumped to his feet, startled. The tails of the dark frock coat whipped about him like a cape. He snapped a guttural a command in a language Speed had never heard.

Something zipped close past Speed's left ear. He pivoted, filling his right hand with his 44.

An Amazon Indian warrior stood on the catwalk! Thickset, more than six-feet tall and clad only in a loincloth and gaudy ceremonial war feathers, his teeth stained black and filed to points, the savage held a blowpipe. He had just fired a dart at Speed, missing by only fractions of an inch; no doubt a curare-tipped poison dart! The savage threw aside the blowpipe, raised a machete and charged with a mighty war whoop.

SPEED BROUGHT up his .44 and shot the Indian in the heart, sending the warrior pitching from the catwalk into the shadows far below. The echo of the shot rolled like thunder around the mighty Zeppelin's interior.

Callas was now shinning his way up the master ring girder, where it rose from the hydrogen cell, using his arms and feet to scale the giant curved ring toward the top of the dirigible.

Speed rushed to a latitudinal catwalk, holstering his pistol. He had purposely aimed for the Indian's upper torso, hoping the man's thickset body would stop the bullet. This was no place to be firing guns. An errant round could cause catastrophe. He reached the shadows where he first saw Callas and found the explosive device, a ticking time bomb with the clock face showing ninety seconds and counting!

Speed had been a demolitions expert during the Great War. He disabled the bomb in an instant, tossing it aside

Callas had gained the top of the ring girder.

Speed shouted, "Callas, what the devil are you doing? Get down here!"

Callas emitted a blood-curdling shout that matched the war cry of the slain Indian. Steadying himself with one arm wrapped around the metal girder, his other hand went beneath his frock coat and emerged with a machete. He began hacking away at the fabric inches above him.

SPEED BOUNDED onto the curved ring girder and started climbing, his sinewy arms and legs propelling him in swift pursuit. He had reached the halfway mark when Callas completed making a large enough gash in the fabric for him to hoist himself through the hole, into the blackness of night.

Men were approaching at a run along the catwalk from the bow of the ship. They wore the uniforms of the Zeppelin crew. Speed followed Callas through the hole, climbing atop the outer skin of the dirigible.

While onboard, the luxury airship had seemed to be sedately cruising along. But the force of the Zeppelin's forward momentum nearly tore loose Speed's grip of the ring girder, as if he were straddling the rooftop of a highballing cross-country freight. The Zeppelin's propellers and engine sounds thrummed loudly.

ON THE CURVATURE of the outer fabric, Callas was plunging his machete into the material, letting his weight and gravity drag him down along the side of the ship, slicing open the fabric as he slid down the airship's circumference, the jagged, wind-flapping gash widening behind him. The little man's eyes were wild in the Zeppelin's flight lights. Callas released the machete and dropped in a freefall, arms extended, venting his warrior's cry. The tails of his black frock coat flapped about him like bat wings. The jungle blackness rushing past below swallowed him.

THE LONG RIP made by the machete was to widening alarmingly.

SPEED WAS SPREADING himself flat against the *Rio's* curvature, so as not to be swept into the tailwind. He repositioned himself, intending to climb back through the tear. The crewmen were shouting in alarm from the catwalk inside.

Then the hydrogen cell exploded in a blinding, incredible orange-red flash that instantly engulfed the dirigible. *Callas had planted a second bomb!* The airship lurched sharply to starboard.

The wildly flapping loose fabric shielded Speed from the searing explosion, but the concussion of the blast swatted him from the airship like a fly and then he was dropping into the smells of the jungle—the stink of decay; animal, vegetation, and human—that drew him into its smothering embrace.

THE CITY of Rio momentarily hung suspended like a giant, fiery bird of legend. Then the majestic ball of fire cascaded earthward.

2

DESCENT INTO HELL

The broad fronds of tall trees broke his fall. The explosion had caused the airship to veer landward, and the arc of Speed's fall cleared him of the river. The canopy of fronds, and the interlocking branches and vines beneath battered him as he plummeted through them, like fighters repeatedly punching, knocking the wind from his lungs. But they slowed his descent. He landed roughly upon the spongy jungle floor.

HE DREW himself to his feet, sore from the beating the tree limbs had given him. But they had saved his life. There were no broken bones. He ran toward the pandemonium he heard from the direction of the river.

The framework of the Zeppelin's tail section was a towering torch that seared the night with garish flame. The _Rio_ had crashed nose first. The passenger gondola was half-submerged, twisted wreckage near the river-bank. Trees lining the river were aflame, illuminating a scene from Dante's *Inferno*. Screams filled the night. Some people were on fire, flinging themselves about in the water, attempting to extinguish the flames. Lifeless bodies were everywhere, some floating downriver where the eyes of waiting crocodiles shone like rubies on the surface of the dark, rushing water.

THEN A HORRIFIC, whooping chant filled the air, and a war party of headhunters sprang from the jungle, descending upon the survivors with a savage, murderous fury. The surviving crewmen of the Zeppelin were discovering that their weapons would not fire because the powder was wet. Men and women who had made it ashore were falling under the blows of stone clubs and machetes.

THE FRAME of the dirigible collapsed upon itself with a great *whoosh!* and then there was scant illumination, which only made louder the pitiable cries for mercy and the victorious whooping of the savages and the *thwack!-thwack!-thwack!* of civilized men and women being clubbed to death with ancient weapons.

Speed angled toward where he saw a young woman was being pinned to the ground by three savages, her faint pleas for help lost beneath the rabble of the surrounding slaughter. One headhunter was wrenching at the poor woman's head while another held her to the ground. The third was hacking at her neck with a stone ax. They never saw Speed coming. He downed the Indians with a trio of well-placed slugs.

THE WOMAN WAS DEAD, partially decapitated. Speed remembered her as Sonya's university roommate, a vivacious girl, full of life.

A WAR CRY spun him around. A wide-eyed savage was charging, his spear upraised. Speed fired again. The bullet blew away part of the Indian's forehead.

Colonel Whittaker, his daughter, and another man--a crewman of the Zeppelin; Speed recalled his name was Chalmers—were cornered close by, fighting for their lives. Sonya stood clutching a big stone in her hands, ready to bash anyone who got close enough. Her father and one of the warriors were battling hand to hand, each gripping the other's throat. The savage was raising his club for the deathblow. Sonya started to assist her father, but the Indian swiped with his club, almost braining her. Chalmers was bobbing and weaving to confuse two Indians who were trying to corner him, one with a spear, the other with a machete.

SPEED CHOSE HIS TARGETS CAREFULLY. The .44 roared. The Indian at the Colonel's throat collapsed, dead. He fired again. The Indian with the spear toppled at Chalmers' feet. The one with the machete roared his rage and charged at Speed. Speed pulled the trigger again. *Click!* Empty.

The warrior fell into the mud, dead. Chalmers had run the man through with the other's tribal spear.

Speed hefted this man's fallen machete, prepared to continue the fight.

But then something strange happened.

The Indians abruptly ceased encircling Speed, Chalmers, the Colonel, and Sonya. Those engaged in mutilating the corpses along the riverbank also halted in their unholy endeavors. As if on cue, the savages faded stealthily, silently back into the jungle, gone as quickly as they had appeared.

CHALMERS SAID, "WELL I'LL BE."

Sonya eyed the direction in which the headhunters had disappeared. She was still holding onto the rock with both hands. "Is it just my imagination or were they scared away?"

The Colonel said, "It's as if they sensed some invisible, silent presence commanding them to withdraw."

Chalmers nodded. "Yeah. As if they were frightened of being caught."

Speed looped the machete through his belt, so the wide blade rode against his left leg for quick access. He reloaded the .44 with fresh cartridges from his gun belt.

"WHICH BEGS THE QUESTION, what would scare off *those* fellows?"

The Colonel said, "At least we've bought ourselves some breathing room."

"Yeah," said Chalmers, "and it looks like we're the only ones."

There was no indication of life along the littered riverbank; no sounds save the sputtering embers of a once great airship's remains and the faint splashing of crocodiles feeding.

SONYA TOSSED THE ROCK ASIDE.

"Mister McCoy, I owe you an apology. You were right and I was so wrong. All of the research I did for Papa was on paper, in books. Reality is so different. This place isn't enchanted at all. It's a land of decay and death. It's a dreadful place. The things we've witnessed…they were chopping off people's heads! My poor friend, Lois…"

The Colonel placed an arm around her shoulders. "There there, my dear. Warfare is never pretty, but it is these savages' acknowledged code combat."

She said in a small voice, "Lois was no warrior."

Speed said, "Unfortunately, those Indians are. They're a warrior society. These tribes love to fight. What the scalp was to the North American Indian, heads are to these fellows. A warrior seeks the *muisak*, the soul of his victim, that they believe is contained in and by the victim's shrunken head. It gives him power in battle."

The rhythmic beating of the jungle drums resumed, seemingly from every direction in the night.

Chalmers stole an appreciative glance at the firm contours of Sonya's figure, clad in damp khaki, then returned his attention to the matter at hand.

"We can't very well stay put. We won't be out of this until I'm holding a cold beer in my hand."

Speed chuckled. He liked this brassy, two-fisted young crewman. Then his eyes grew grim.

"Let's take a look at what's left of the *Rio*. There were lifeboats onboard. There's a slim chance we can find something that will float us back to that rubber plantation we flew over awhile ago."

Sonya drew a clenched hand to her mouth. "Don't think poorly of me, but…I simply couldn't bear to walk down among that horror…could I wait with Mr. Chalmers?"

Chalmers' handsome, grime-smudged face cracked with a cocksure grin.

"No need to accompany them, miss, if you don't want to." He gestured with the spear he held. "You're safe next to Jake Chalmers of West Allis, Wisconsin. We can keep your father and Speed in sight from here. Er, right, gentlemen?" His hopefulness would have been comical under less dire circumstances.

Speed said, "Sounds good, Jake, if that's what the lady wants. Coming, Colonel?"

"At your side, old man."

They advanced on the river, angling toward the densest concentration of wreckage, walking amid black shapes in the mud that could only be the corpses of those either instantly crushed on impact or butchered by the Indians. Amid the grisly scene were grotesquely mundane items etched in the moonlight; a man's sporty cap, a parasol, a magazine, the lower plate of a set of false teeth, bloodied and half buried in the muck.

SPEED SAID, "HERE, WHAT'S THIS?"

He retrieved a battery-powered lantern, its glass plate cracked, half missing. But the bulb inside was intact. He flicked the switch. The lantern's stark electrical beam swept the riverbank.

The Colonel growled his displeasure at what the light revealed. "Nothing we can use. Blast the luck."

A violent rustling sound suddenly erupted in the darkness behind them.

Sonya Whittaker's scream of pure naked terror cut through the night like a bayonet ripping human flesh.

3

Speed and the Colonel pelted in the direction of the scream. The sound of a fierce struggle was replaced by a gurgling, slurping, sub- or semi-human gibbering that rapidly receded into the night.

The Colonel actually overtook Speed.

"Sonya!"

Speed threw the lantern's beam across a grisly sight.

Chalmers lay flat on his back. His feet were hammering upon the ground. The spear lay at his side, snapped in half. His hands gripped his stomach. Thick, syrupy gore bubbled out between his fingers like spilled red chili from a wound that was gaping enough for Speed to glimpse white bone and pulsating organs.

Speed dropped to a knee.

"Chalmers…what—?"

Blood bubbled from the corners of Chalmers' mouth. He said, weakly, "They took Sonya...lizard men..."

WHITTAKER GASPED. "Lizard men? Sonya? Why, don't you see, McCoy, the poor devil's hallucinating!"

Speed said, "Then where is she? Chalmers, we'll track them down, whatever or whoever they are. What else you can tell us?"

Chalmers reached up and grasped Speed's shoulder in a vise-like grip, summoning dwindling strength to form one word.

"Callas..."

Speed leaned in closer. "Callas? He was with them?"

The tapping of Chalmers' boot heels was growing faint. He coughed. He managed to say, "Callas *rules* them!" Then his grip loosened from Speed's shoulder. His arm dropped away.

Chalmers was dead.

Whittaker wore a stunned expression. "We've got to get my daughter back!"

Speed swept the electric lantern's beam across damp ground that indicated a violent struggle to his trained eye. Indentations of high-heeled shoes that he'd noticed Sonya wearing were discernable; their jagged scars in the ground indicated that she had been dragged before being lifted off her feet. There were crazy sweeps in the mud, as if made by large, sweeping tails, and what looked like the impressions of lizard feet. Big lizards, and a passel of them.

WHITTAKER APPEARED unaware of the weird nature of the imprints. Speed saw no reason to further agitate him so he said only, "They've gone upriver. We're not but a few minutes behind."

"We can follow them?"

Speed had once served as a tracker for the Texas Rangers, but could he read signs at night in the smothering denseness of a rainforest?

HE SAID, "LET'S GO!" and took off at a loping run, the electric lantern held in one hand, his pistol in the other, following the lizard prints interspersed with the tail sweeps.

COLONEL WHITTAKER HUFFED ALONG CLOSELY behind him, displaying a robust vitality for a man his age.

After a quarter mile, the trail angled inland and became more difficult to read. The crowns of towering liana-festooned trees intertwined a hundred feet or more above the ground, blocking out the moonlight.

The relentless jungle drums never ceased.

Speed and the Colonel encountered as much swampland as there was firm ground. The luminous finger of the lantern's beam guided them, revealing a bent or broken twig here, a disturbed clump of vines there; traces where the ground was too hard to read, and then a stitch of her clothing fabric clinging to a vine, or some other sign that would put Speed back on the track.

THEN THE JUNGLE opened up and there was the river again, running past an Indian village that basked silently in the moonlight. At least twenty native huts stood haphazardly arranged with a much larger circular, communal hut in the center. The town appeared deserted.

SPEED AND WHITTAKER APPROACHED CAUTIOUSLY.

The village was as it appeared. The cooking fires were still warm. Canoes were tethered to the bank. But nothing living was present here. A tree bore obscene fruit. Eight recently decapitated heads were strung to the branches with pliable bark ropes passed through the mouths and out the necks.

Speed and the Colonel paused at the far edge of the village.

Speed said, "The ones who have Sonya passed through here. The village was empty when they came."

Whittaker's brow furrowed. "Now how the deuce can you tell that?"

"Well for starters, we haven't found any bodies chewed up like poor Chalmers."

"You think the Indians of this village went into hiding?"

"Warriors don't hide. They've moved their families to safety, which indicates that they didn't withdraw from the river before out of fear. They had something planned and got sidetracked when the *Rio* crashed in their backyard. Those drums would tell us if we could decipher what they're saying."

They pushed on.

The nighttime heat was almost overpowering. The damp air was leaden. The ground underfoot was an unbroken expanse of thick, clinging, evil-smelling mud. The Colonel stumbled several times from near exhaustion. At some point, he had lost his pith helmet. Speed used his machete to hack their way through the nearly impenetrable tangles of creeper vines that were ripe with parasitic orchids. Then the ground became firm because it was rising.

And soon they were standing upon a ridge that overlooked a sweeping valley and the ghostly sprawl of an ancient city of stone!

Its maze of ruins, ravaged by time and the encroaching jungle, was a moss-covered, vine-strewn labyrinth in the moonlight, dominated by a tall, formidable, incredibly well-preserved structure that was side-stepped and flat-topped with exterior spiral steps and ramps.

COLONEL WHITTAKER GASPED. "I *knew* it! Great Scott, McCoy, do you see how close we were to *this*? A ziggurat in better condition than any I've seen of the Aztecs or the Mayans!" His hushed voice was constricted with awe. "The ancient Babylonians and Assyrians had them, y'know, but their origin is lost in the mists of prehistoric time. It's been a lifetime passion of mine. I know their interior layout, everything. In theory, of course."

Speed pointed toward a golden sliver of illumination that shone weakly at the base of the structure.

"What's that?"

"Why...the ziggurat is inhabited! This is where they've taken Sonya, isn't it?"

Speed said, "Let's find out."

They entered the maze of ancient ruins that surrounded the looming structure. The Colonel was visibly reinvigorated. Speed had memorized the maze from higher ground and before long the course he'd plotted took them to the base of the ziggurat. They advanced on the sliver of gold, which proved to be illumination seeping out from behind a heavy stone door that was ajar.

Speed handed Whittaker his revolver. "Here,

Colonel." He hefted the machete that was hanging from his belt. "Good luck."

"McCoy, I just want to say that I appreciate what you're doing, risking your life for my daughter. This whole tragedy is my fault. My misguided enthusiasm! I should have never—"

"WE'VE GOT a job to do, Colonel. Let's hope we're not walking into a trap."

Speed passed through the doorway. Colonel Whittaker followed closely. A squeaking, scampering sound drew their attention. A rat the size of a small dog withdrew belligerently from the presence of human intruders.

The constant thumping of jungle drums did not carry into this musty, cool place. Instead, though, came a faint but noticeable humming that vibrated the walls, the floor, the very atmosphere.

Whittaker muttered, "Queer sound, that."

"It's coming from this direction."

They followed a winding, musty passage for a distance before arriving at a shallow flight of rough-hewn stairs that led down to a heavy wooden door. The strange, vibrating hum, a constant monotone, had grown ominously loud. It originated from behind the wooden door. They went down the steps.

Speed inched the door open a crack and peered through. He crouched to provide the Colonel with a clear view.

A close, swampy stench assailed their nostrils. It was a large, square, low, vaulted cavern. Smooth walls hewn from solid rock, draped with ancient tapestries, illuminated by scores of tall candles.

The low semi-human hum was now a bone-shivering drone, part murmur, part drooling, slobbering sounds from the dozens of vile creatures crowded into the cavern, bowing with their eyes downcast. They possessed the slimy, muscular, predatory bodies of giant lizards—weighing perhaps two hundred pounds each!--while the moist, droning hum of their slithering tongues had a weird, unsettling human quality, that ability to repeat the incantations of the robed, cowled figure who stood over a raised rectangular slab of stone surrounded by tapestries at this end of the cavern, not thirty feet from the door.

Sonya Whittaker was lashed to the altar. Her shapely body was clad now only in the remnants of silken undergarments after the ordeal of her abduction. She writhed in a futile attempt to escape

The shaman's back was to the cavern. His hands were raised. In one hand he held a long-bladed dagger. His incantations were rising into a frenzied crescendo, as was the sibilant murmuring of his unholy congregation.

4

It was a nightmare reality; semi-human monsters that could only be some offshoot on the branch of evolution, some genetic travesty unchecked since the world's infancy when Creation was an experiment.

Speed and the Colonel drew away from the door.

Speed whispered, "We're sort of outnumbered. We'll have to do this fast."

The Colonel was slack-jawed. "Do *what* fast? B'ghad, what are those *things* in there?"

"Your ascended masters of wisdom. Colonel, there's no time for talk. Those creatures are to be preoccupied in a prayer of some sort, but that's not going to last."

"TELL ME WHAT TO DO, McCoy. I would give my life—"

"Let's hope it doesn't come to that. Okay, here's how we work it. We sidle along the wall to the altar.

31

The shaman has his back to us. At my signal, use candles to torch the tapestry. It's our only chance. This place is a thousand years old if it's a day, so it should go up like dry hay, which should get those lizard boys to hopping. Use the gun on the shaman, and cover me. I'll use the machete on Sonya's ropes and on anyone who tries to get stand in our way."

They slipped inside and crept furtively on the balls of their feet, their backs to the wall. The close, swampy stench made it almost impossible to breathe. Speed held the machete low at his side so its gleam would not reflect candlelight, so as not to distract the attention of the bowing, devoutly murmuring creatures.

Speed took hold of one candleholder with his free hand. The Colonel did the same.

Speed had hoped to get within ten feet of the altar before initiating his plan, but with twenty feet to go, the shaman suddenly stopped his chanting and looked down into Sonya's eyes, which were fixed on her father and Speed as they advanced. She was biting her quivering, ripe lower lip to keep from crying out but the shaman saw the surprise in her terrified eyes. He whirled to confront the intruders.

Speed was not surprised to behold the sinister countenance of Juan Callas.

Callas hissed a command in some unknowable tongue, arousing his "congregation."

Dozens of lizard men raised their heads as one. Nearly a hundred beady eyes shone with sadistic malevolence in the candlelight. Tongues slithering. Semi-human grunts gurgled. They began to advance.

In unison, Speed and the Colonel hurled their candles at the draperies. Speed's candle ignited fabric around the altar. The Colonel's candle flared up drapery decorating one of the cavern walls, instantly igniting the antique material.

The nearest lizard men continued to advance on all fours, their eyes shining blood red in the flames, their teeth bared and snapping, tongues searching for something to lash, not advancing with the natural swiftness of lizards, but with the caution born of a reasoning, calculating, cunning intelligence.

The Colonel fired two rounds that exploded one lizard head, then another. The nearest creatures checked their advance.

Speed rushed to the altar. He hacked at the ropes bonding Sonya, freeing her. She flung her scantily clad body against his and started to gush something in gratitude. He interrupted her by drawing her behind him with his left arm, shielding her with his body.

Callas was using his dagger to gesture wildly, exhorting his creatures with more commands in that strange sibilant tongue. A chorus of squeals from near an adjacent wall indicated that the flames were roasting some of the creatures there, causing confusion.

The Colonel took aim at Callas.

Two feather-tipped arrows struck Callas squarely in the chest before Whittaker could fire. Callas's eyes and mouth formed circles of surprise. He dropped the dagger and stumbled into the flames.

Whittaker rushed to join Speed and Sonya. "What the devil—?"

His words were drowned out by a chorus of piercing, bloodcurdling war whoops that erupted from a stream of headhunters that came storming through the doorway, attacking the startled lizard men with a blood-spraying assault of swinging stone axes and clubs and machetes and bows and arrows, a mad symphony of battle cries and slavering gore as the Lizard Men fought back.

Sonya pressed herself against Speed as if embracing life itself. "I don't understand!"

"This is what the drumming was about," said Speed. "We came along on the night the Indians had banded together to turn on Callas and these lizard men. That's why the village was deserted. The Indians hid their families in case of reprisal."

A crackling orange-red flame was spreading throughout the cavern, filling it with smoke and the stench of roasting flesh.

SONYA AVERTED her eyes from the hellish carnage.

"We're going to die, aren't we? We're trapped. We'll never escape!"

Her father was studying the base of the altar.

"I wouldn't be too sure about that, my dear. You know, I am an authority on ziggurats." Whittaker spoke with enthusiasm as if elucidating for his sycophants aboard the *City of Rio*, not cornered here with searing flames and bloody slaughter closing in from every direction. He absently returned the pistol to Speed. "There should be a lever of some sort. The shaman would create a puff of smoke or some such, you see, to stage a dramatic exit and…ah, here it is! And I daresay it's seen recent use."

He reached for a stone protrusion at the bottom end of the altar. But before he could touch it, a whistling arrow struck in Whittaker in the back, embedding half its length in him.

SONYA SCREAMED. "PAPA, *NO!!!*"

Whittaker crumpled.

Speed peered across the altar. The slaughter between Indians and lizard men raged on. It was impossible to tell which savage in the melee had fired the arrow. He brushed a shirtsleeve across his eyes to wipe away the sweat. The primal heat of unfettered bloodlust and the flames were making the cavern hot as the inside of an oven.

"GOT ME THROUGH THE LUNG!" The Colonel was trying to extend his hand to touch the stone lever.

Speed said, "Show me how it works, Colonel. Sonya and I will each take you by the arm. We'll fight our way out of this. No one gets left behind."

"I DO, THIS TIME," said Whittaker. "It's my fault we're here, and I'm paying the price."

Sonya knelt beside him. "Papa, you mustn't talk that way. You're coming with us."

"Child, I have much to answer for. More than twenty people died when our Zeppelin went down. Go now." Whittaker's glassy gaze shifted to Speed. "I'm asking you, McCoy, man to man. I've lived my life. Sonya deserves the chance to live hers. See to it, won't you?"

Speed was about to offer his assurance when the Colonel thrashed in a final death spasm. His hand lifted with his dying breath. The hand fell upon the stone lever. The floor vanished beneath Speed and Sonya and suddenly they were falling, falling, falling down an oversized tube beneath an opened trap door!

The skirmish in the cavern, the flames and the death, abruptly ceased to exist for them as gravity whisked them along. Speed managed to retain hold of the machete and his pistol. Then they were sent flying from the tube as if being spat out of the snout of some giant beast.

Speed sprang to his feet. They were outdoors, at the foot of the mighty ziggurat. The ruins of the ancient city surrounding them were limned in the soft shadings of moonlight.

Sonya winced, steadying herself on one shapely leg.

"I've twisted my ankle!"

A sibilant purr came from the darkness: "Oh, that shan't be a problem, my dear. You're not going anywhere, either of you."

Juan Callas emerged from the shadows, adorned in his shaman robes. He appeared unaffected by the arrows that had struck him.

Speed brought up his revolver.

"Callas, you're a sorcerer. I've seen enough to believe it. You and your *things* have been terrorizing the Indian tribes in this region." He thought of the machete-wielding, dart-blowing savage who had assisted Callas in sabotaging the Zeppelin. "How long have you been playing these tribes off against each other to consolidate your power?"

"For centuries," said Callas. He looked dangerous precisely because of his slight stature; an evil gnome with a crafty, malignant gleam in his beady eyes. "And it will not end tonight. There is no stopping my power."

"I am impressed," said Speed. "Your powers include being able to go from this," he gestured to the moss-covered ruins, "to high society in Rio. You were never interested in the Colonel or in his pet theories that weren't so wild after all."

Sonya said, "It was about me. You wanted to get *me* out here?"

Callas inclined his head, the slightest nod. "Since I first encountered you at that ball at the governor's mansion. A blood sacrifice is required, you see, to appease our gods. You are the chosen one, Miss Whittaker. I cultivated your father and encouraged this expedition solely to draw you here for the honor of sacrifice."

Speed said, "Spare us the malarkey. This girl's father died thinking he was paying a blood debt, that he responsible for the *Rio* going down and all those people dying. Callas, you're the one responsible. The Indian tribes banded together and disrupted your sacrifice. And I'm escorting Miss Whittaker back to Rio. There's just one last thing I need to take care of."

Callas smirked. "You are referring, I presume, to your death."

"Hardly, short stuff. It's *your* party that's over."

Callas regarded the revolver in Speed's hand. He laughed.

"You'll need to do better than that. Do you think mere bullets can harm me? I am three thousand years old."

Speed holstered his pistol. "You're right. When in Rome."

Callas frowned. He said, "Rome?"

Speed said, "Tell your gods I said hello and good-bye," and with one swift swipe of the machete, he neatly decapitated Callas.

The little man's head toppled from his shoulders like a ball knocked from its display mantle. The head-- eyes still beady, the mouth still smirking--rolled off into the darkness.

But Callas did not fall over dead. He remained

standing. There was no blood. He was no longer Juan Callas.

A lizard head emerged from the cavity of his neck like some hideous slow-motion jack-in-the-box. What had been a man dropped forward onto all fours upon the ground, arms and legs refiguring himself into reptilian form. The robes fell away and the human features dissolved until only a grotesquely large lizard remained, its slimy skin glossy in the moonlight. The only human trait remaining was the same crafty, malignant evil that had gleamed in the eyes of Juan Callas.

Speed told the lizard, "Here's another cliché for you. There's more than one way to skin a cat—or a lizard."

The lizard darted for him, coming in for the kill, a deadly blur.

And just as fast, Speed used both hands to swing the machete in two broad strokes, making a big X that quartered the giant lizard. The four chunks of lizard meat separated from each other but palpitated upon the ground like fish slapping themselves to death on a pier. Speed took another swing that lopped off the lizard's head. The creature's tongue lay like a small snake that had died crawling halfway into its mouth, but the head continued to oddly quiver as if infused with jolts of electricity.

Speed kicked the lizard head away from the other pieces.

"Something tells me we'd better move out before

humpty-dumpty here puts himself back together again."

Sonya was pretending to ignore the fact that the skimpy silk adorning her figure left nothing to the imagination.

"But...how? We're stranded in the middle of nowhere!"

"We're a twenty minute run from a deserted Indian village. The village is on the river. We'll steal a canoe. The river will take us to the rubber plantation."

Sonya smiled bravely. The intelligence and discipline that had gained her father's respect as a research assistant shone through, and Speed found this inner quality every bit as attractive as her physical charms.

She took a step and winced again.

"Run? I'm sorry, Mr. McCoy, but with this twisted ankle I'm afraid I can barely walk."

He secured the machete through his belt, freeing his left arm.

"Call me Speed," he suggested. "We're about to become very well acquainted."

He threw her across his broad left shoulder, grinning at her gasp of surprise.

Then, with Sonya Whittaker held securely in place, Speed broke into a steady trot that took them away from there.

II

FRAGGED: A MCCALL & TARA
MYSTERY

FRAGGED

Vietnam. 1970. Quang Ngai Province, north of Saigon.

The Huey gunship banked in over Firebase Tiger, a clearing carved from the jungle hilltop.

The woman, who was calling herself Tara Carpenter, began snapping pictures from the open side door of the helicopter, from behind the shoulder of the door gunner and his big M-60 machine gun.

The landing zone was a barren five acres. After the stark green carpet of jungle they'd flown over from Saigon, the base was drab and squalid. There were no trees, no color except for the coating of dust that blanketed everything: bunkers, vehicles and personnel. Machine gun emplacements were at intervals along the perimeter. Artillery and morTara were inside the compound. The sun, like an angry red ball seen

43

through the gauze of a humid haze' was arcing low in the west, painting the horizon beyond the tree line a brilliant red.

The view of this remote scene vanished behind a veil of red dust a sandstorm kicked up by the choppers' backwash as the pilot touched the Huey down gently on the helo pad and initiated systems shutdown.

Tara's fellow passenger stood beside her.

Getting enough pretty pictures for the war protestors?" he asked.

His name was Cord McCall He was an investigator assigned to a special operations unit of the Joint Services Criminal Investigation Division detachment in Saigon. Death was naturally commonplace in a war zone, but there were other crimes perpetrated within military ranks--homicide, desertion, robbery-- that fell, under the d jurisdiction. McCall, a Major was forty years old, dark-haired& heavily muscled. His fatigues were sharply pressed even in the three-digit heat and suffocating humidity.

He did not wait for a response, but leaped from the gunship and strode toward a trio of awaiting soldiers,

Tara hopped to the ground and caught up with him. She was seven years McCall junior, a redhead with intelligent green eyes that could glitter like those of a mischievous cat. Her GI fatigues did nothing to conceal a trim, shapely figure chose not to respond to his sarcasm because, McCall knew, she well under-stood and appreciated its source.

First off, he was not overjoyed with being assigned

the dual task of performing his normal duties in addition to nurse-maiding a journalist. But there was another, more significant reason for his displeasure with the presence of Tara Carpenter in Vietnam, and she and he were the only two people in Nam or anywhere else who could appreciate the true undercurrent of tension that had crackled between them since he'd met her, as ordered, at the Saigon airport that morning.

Tan and Cord were husband and wife

Therein lay one hell of a tale, somehow as simple as it was complex. she'd been Cord's wife for three years before he was sent to Sam. Tara had never been your average military base wife. She'd begun free-lancing her photographs to wire services and news magazines before they met. cord was supportive of her career and, during their separation while he was in Vietnam, she continued to rise through the ranks of professional photographers.

He had been dumbstruck when he met her at the airport, not having had the slightest hunch that the photojournalist assigned to him was his own wife! She confided in him right off. It had taken considerable finagling on her part, she'd told him, including coming up with a cockamamie story for her editor about the need for a cover name, and she'd pulled it off. Wars were the stuff that Pulitzer Prizes were made of. But ambition and self-interest were not the only reasons she had hustled this assignment, she quickly assured him.

She had come because of love. She'd grown impatient, sitting on the sidelines in the States. She wanted to learn for herself what was going on "in country, as the soldiers called it. She wanted to experience her husband's world. She would not have interfered under normal circumstances, she insisted, but this war was hardly normal. As his wife, she well knew of his strength and his self-confidence. Now, she explained, she yearned to know its source.

Cord was anything but happy about the situation but he tentatively agreed to maintain her secret, that she was his spouse, as much to avoid complications as to avoid complications as to avoid appearing the fool. He made no secret of his displeasure during the drive from the airport. He was irritated by her presence. In addition to his concern for her safety, he had to keep his mind on his work, he'd groused. He hadn't bothered mentioning the pure sexual charge she always felt whenever she was nearby, which would be a major distraction during their "assignment" together. He hoped that he could keep his hots for Tara under wraps. But he couldn't deny it, and that in itself could lead to complications.

He protested adamantly, in her presence, to his commanding officer, who'd gone on to not-so-patiently re-explained to McCall how this was part of a PR campaign the Pentagon was waging in the hope that, by providing first-hand reports from Vietnam, they would be able to maintain the morale, hearts and minds of the American people.

That said McCall was issued this assignment to Firebase Tiger and Tara accompanied him.

When he and Tara now crossed the short distance from the Huey to the three waiting soldiers.

Their ranking member stepped forward. "Major McCall, I'm Captain Larson, Executive Officer in Charge. Welcome to Firebase Tiger."

Larson was built like a fanner, thirtyish, with a sunburned crew cut and the leathery skin and flinty eyes of a much older man. He did not salute, as was the Custom in a combat zone. Enemy snipers loved to disrupt the chain of command, and seeing who were saluted made selecting targets easy for them. Therefore, saluting was avoided outdoors.

"Thank YOU! Captain, but to tell YOU the truth, I'd just as soon be somewhere else.

The man next to Larson grunted. He was a big black man with H-b stripes on his sleeve. That goes for every mother's son in this hell hale, sir."

"Easy, Top," said Larson. "Sir, this is Sergeant Hines. He's my top shirt.

"I know I said McCall, "I studied your personnel files."

The third man was a First Lieutenant named Grey and everything about him matched his name. Blond-haired! in his late twenties, there was a paleness to him that was almost albino-like. He exuded jittery nervousness. McCall had seen Cases of battle fatigue and he recognized those symptoms now.

"Captain, Sergeant Hines is only speaking the

truth." There was a tremor to Grey's voice. I wish I'd never heard of Firebase Tiger.

McCall said, "I'm here because you have a fragged colonel."

"Had, sir," said Larson. "Lieutenant Colonel Emmett, 13th Infantry Battalion. Someone tossed a hand grenade into his hooch just before dawn today and splashed the walls with his guts."

"Hooch" was fl slang for makeshift living quarters. "Fragging" was another recently coined term. Bad command decisions by an officer often got good soldiers killed. Sometimes an officer's own men-- considering it mare an act of survival than murder-- would toss a grenade to a hooch, blowing such an officer into itty bitty officer fragments--"frag" him in other words--before the officer could get anyone else killed.

"Where's the body now?

"What was left," said Larson was tagged and bagged and returned to Saigon on the daily chopper run at 1700 hours.

Hines eyed McCall speculatively. to thing you better know up front, sir. Don't expect anyone here to feel too bad about what happened to the Colonel."

Grey cleared his throat again. He nodded at Tara. 'Uh if you don't mind, Major, who's she?"

"Her?" McCall spoke offhandedly. 'Names Carpenter. Pretend she's not here. I do. Okay, Captain, show me where the Colonel got fragged."

Acting as if she had not heard Tara commenced taking pictures of these grouped men.

Activity swirled around them a male world of coarse language, exhaust fumes and the clicking and clanking of engines, equipment and weaponry. Nearly every soldier was toting an M-16 and a wary attitude, eyeing the jungle beyond the cut-down fire zone outside the perimeter where the shadows of encroaching night were deepening.

"The Colonel got it in his hooch," said Larson. "It's next to the main bunker."

He led them toward a squalid, dust covered pile of sandbags that was somewhat bigger than the other hooches.

The Colonel's hooch was a low, ten-by-twelve, makeshift structure of timber and plywood beneath a shell at sandbags. Its entrance was charred, misshapen from the outward force of the murderous blast.

McCall crouched for a few seconds to observe the interior. The walls had indeed been splashed with blood. Flies buzzed, thick and loud. He stood and faced the others.

"Did anyone see anything?"

Larson shook his head, negative. "Security was paying attention to outside the perimeter. Everyone heard the blast. The nearest ones to the site were me, Sergeant Hines and the Lieutenant

Hines nodded. "Cap and I were sprucing up the files for the Inspector General's visit day after tomorrow. If it hadn't been for a couple of walls between the colonel's hooch and the TOC, we'd have been hamburger too."

Grey indicated a squad-sized hooch across from the Tactical Operations command bunker. "Those are the officers' quarters. We compared notes after it happened. No one saw anything."

"It wasn't the VC," said Larson confidently. "They'd never breach our perimeter."

"Any ideas then," said Mc "on who'd want the Colonel dead bad enough to f rag him?"

"You mean suspects?" Larson nodded, the flint cold in his eyes. "Yeah, I could think of a few."

Grey cleared his throat, a nervous habit preceding almost anything he said. "You might as well go ahead and tell him, Cap."

Tara lowered her camera, "Tell us what?"

This got McCall's goat. "Not us, ma'am. Me." He returned his attention to the men, "I take it the Colonel was not well liked.!!

Hines chuckled coarsely. "You're saying that lust because someone fragged his ass to hell, right?"

"The Colonel was assigned here last month. A new CO always shakes up a command to put his own brand on it. The troops never like it, but it usually settles into mutual respect after awhile, sort of a honeymoon in reverse.

Tara murmured beneath her breath, Now there's a concept.

Hines grunted. "You want a list of suspects, Major?

You could start with the roster of every man assigned to this base." 12

Grey cleared his throat. "There are thirty men who were stationed here who have been dropped from that list. And I should be one of them. I should have been Out there with Sergeant Williams and his platoon last night."

"Lieutenant Grey is a platoon leader with Bravo company" Larson explained. "A platoon from Bravo company was ambushed last night on patrol, Heavy casualties."

"Fifteen killed, fifteen wounded," said Hines. "Wiped out by one of our own bombs. The VC find our dud shells, rig them up and use them against us."

McCall next went around the hooch to the entrance of the command center. He glanced inside. Tactical maps were spread out upon folding tables, Rifle and a crates served as chairs. A clerk was busy at a typewriter. A radio man monitored mostly static from a small receiver.

McCall turned back to Larson "Let me guess. Saigon promised you replacements! but night's falling and they're not here yet."

Larson nodded bleakly. "And until they get here, we're way short of manpower. I'm hoping Charlie hasn't figured that out yet.

"Issue me an M-1 said McCall. "You've got at least one replacement.'

"Two, actually," Tara volunteered.

They ignored her.

McCall didn't miss the flash of anger that made her eyes a deeper shade of green.

Without clearing his throat, Grey said, "The Colonel should never have ordered us into that sector."

This firebase is assigned two companies of light infantry Larson told McCall. "One supports the other. The line company conducts recon patrols around the base, and it was Bravo Company's turn on the rotation schedule, The other company provides mortar and artillery support from here.

"Go ahead, Major McCall." Lieutenant Grey spoke fervently. "Check my record. I'd have never sent a platoon down those trails where the Colonel ordered me to. I'm not some wet behind the ears cherry That ambush wasn't my fault. Me and sergeant Williams always brought our guys home. Right, Captain?

Larson nodded uncomfortably, "Right, Lieutenant."

Hines said, not unkindly, in an almost paternal voice, "I'd advise you to chill out, Lieutenant, if you don't mind my saying so, sir. You, uh, haven't felt right since, well, since last night. Maybe you ought to lay down in your hooch, sir. I'll have a medic check in with you."

"I don't need a medic, said Grey. "I need to get something off my chest. My father."

McCall frowned. "Your father?"

Tara's knuckles were white around her camera. With one sideways glanced, McCall could tell that an impulse within her was trying to dissuade her from capturing, for posterity, Grey's vulnerability and emotional unbalance; a poignant portrait of the 13

eyes a deeper shade of green.

Without clearing his throat, Grey said, "The Colonel should never have ordered us into that sector."

This firebase is assigned two companies of light infantry Larson told McCall. "One supports the other. The line company conducts recon patrols around the base, and it was Bravo Company's turn on the rotation schedule, The other company provides mortar and artillery support from here.

11 ahead, Major McCall." Lieutenant Grey spoke fervently. "Check my record. I'd have never sent a platoon down those trails where the Colonel ordered me to. I'm not some wet behind the ears cherry That ambush wasn't my fault. Me and sergeant Williams always brought our guys home. Right, captain?

Larson nodded uncomfortably, "Right, Lieutenant."

Hines said, not unkindly, in an almost paternal voice, "I'd advise you to chill out, Lieutenant, if you don't mind my saying so, sir. You, uh, haven't felt right since, well, since last night. Maybe you ought to lay down in your hooch, sir. I'll have a medic check in with you."

"I don't need a medic, said Grey. "I need to get something off my chest. My father."

McCall frowned. "Your father?"

Tara's knuckles were white around her camera. With one sideways glanced, McCall could tell that an impulse within her was trying to dissuade her from capturing, for posterity, Grey's vulnerability and emotional unbalance; a poignant portrait of the ravages of war on even a trained, competent man. Tara grimaced, raised her camera and snapped a picture.

Grey cleared his throat. "The Sergeant I just mentioned, the one who died in the ambush."

"Williams," said McCall. "What about him?"

"He was in the Korean war," said Grey, "and until yesterday he was here! keeping alive officers like me and guys who should have been back home drinking beer. Every man on the base respected Sergeant Williams. He was our teacher, our preacher, the one we looked up to. nut I awed him a personal debt. That's why I wish to God that *I* was a dead man, not him."

"Lieutenant," said Larson, "you followed SOP every step of the way last night. You are not responsible for what happened.

McCall asked Grey, "What does this have to do with your father?"

"Sergeant Williams and my dad served together in Korea," said Grey. "He saved Dad's life. Sarge greased a Red Chinese who was about to run Dad through with a bayonet. They stayed in touch after the war. They were both lifers. I must have heard the story a hundred times growing up. I never got tired of it. Cancer got Dad in '68. I was raised to be a soldier. I couldn't believe my luck when I got assigned to Sergeant Williams. I was supposed to be the platoon leader, but we all knew who kept us alive." Grey's lower lip trembled. "And as his platoon leader, sending him and those men on that patrol last night, I am responsible for the death of the man who saved my fathers life. I stayed behind to get paperwork squared away for the IG. Paperwork, for chrissake! I should have been out there with my men. God forgive me."

Tara stepped forward and rested a hand gently on his shoulder.

"In no way is that true, Lieutenant. Listen to your Captain and to Sergeant Hines. You've been through hell. There is a thing called survivor's guilt. You must maintain. That is what you owe Sergeant Williams and your father and yourself.'

Grey's lower lip stopped trembling. His jaw line regained its prominence. "Yes ma'am. You re right." He chuckled self-consciously. 'What's the old line about not seeing the woods for the trees? Damn straight. I'm not doing anybody any good, pissing and whining about what happened. I've got to recharge my batteries and get ready for whatever's coming at us next."

She nodded. "1 couldn't have said it better myself."

Grey turned to Larson. "Sir, uh, I guess I should try and get some rest."

"I think you're right, Lieutenant

Grey looked in Tara's direction. "Thanks, ma He strode off in the direction of the officers' hooch.

"There goes a fine soldier," said Larson, "wearing a hair shirt from hell."

"He'll make it," said Hines. He said to Tara, "Thank you, ma'am. That boy has a lot to offer this man's army, but he was on the verge of losing it, You helped tilt the scales in the right direction."

Tara began to speak.

McCall spoke before she could. "Yes, ma am. That was humane and noble, and thank you for it. Their eyes connected. "But now 'will ask you to back off again and allow me to get on with this investigation He glanced back at the XO. I want a look at Sergeant Williams hooch."

This way, Larson started them toward a line of hooches near a row of mortar placements. "Mind if I ask! Major, what you think you'll find in Sergeant Williams' hooch that could shed light on what happened to the colonel?"

Striding apace Tara again volunteered.

"I read it this way. The Lieutenant said the men on this base looked up to Sergeant Williams like a hero,"

Hines nodded- "That's as good a word as any, and that's why everyone really hated the colonel after the sarge died." A smile of dawning awareness creased his black features. "And there's your connection. Lady, you're a regular Sherlock Holmes.!!

"She's also a civilian," said McCall. "I'll thank you, Miss Carpenter, to just zip it and take your pictures."

"Understood, General."

McCall sighed. "Sarcasm yet. I be lucky to make colonel with you bird-dogging me." As they drew up before one of the hooches near the morTara, he noted, "Not the quietest neighborhood."

"No such thin as a quiet neighborhood in this

sector," said Hines. "We're surrounded by bogey land. Its zone everywhere beyond that perimeter."

"The first change the Colonel made," said Larson, "was to send out more patrols, and after dark. That was unnecessary too risky. Everyone except the Colonel knew it. The mission for this firebase is recon. You can't do much recon at night. The ambush last night was proof of that

Hines spat derisively. "This base has an outstanding record for targeting VC for our flyboys. We do our job. But doing our job wasn't good enough for the Colonel, that is as long as he didn't have to get off his fat ass in the TOC bunker. He wanted the line companies to go right in and get a higher enemy body count so he could get himself a general's star, and he didn't give a damn about sacrificing soldiers like Sergeant Williams to do it."

Tara raised her camera and snapped a picture of Hines' resignation, weariness and anger.

McCall crouched down and stepped into Sergeant Williams' hooch. Tara lowered her camera and positioned herself between Hines and Larson to observe.

Their grouped presence in the hooch doorway deepened the gloom of its interior. The hooch was of uniform furnishings cot, a foot locker, a makeshift desk.

McCall knelt on one knee and conducted a thorough search of the locker. "uh huh he said triumphantly. He rose, letting the lid of the locker snap shut, and left the hooch, rejoining them, thoughtfully leafing through a bound, leather volume.

Larson tried to see it there was printing on the book's spine. "What did you find, Major?"

Hines guessed, "A Bible?"

McCall shook his head, snapping the book shut. "Not even close

Tara studied the book's dimensions and appearance. 'A diary."

"When men keep one," said McCall pointedly, "its called a journal."

Larson ran a palm across the bristle of his crew cut. "Why would Sergeant Williams keep a journal?"

"Why the hell wouldn't he?" growled Hines. "I'll bet he had plenty of stories to tell, going way back to Korea."

"Too bad he kept them to himself," said Larson. He stretched out a hand, palm up. "Mind if I take a look? Maybe he wrote something about Firebase Tiger."

McCall slid the book into a pocket of his fatigues. "That's what I'm thinking. Sorry Captain, but first I want to have a look for myself "

Tara studied McCall.

"You think Sergeant Williams' diary--excuse me, journal--could hold a clue to who fragged the Colonel."

"I intend to find out"

"1'll show you where the guest billets are," offered Hines, "for what they're worth."

"And it's past chow time," added Larson. "Will you be joining us?"

"Thanks, but no for me." McCall patted the book in his pocket. "Something tells me that this is going to make for interesting reading. I want to get started."

* * *

Tara let herself into one of the guest billets--not her own--without announcing her arrival.

She didn't need to.

McCall sat at a makeshift desk, a slab of plywood resting across two empty oil drums. Remaining seated, he pivoted with incredible speed, a blur of movement, freezing with the .45 in straight-armed target acquisition. He held his fire when he realized that the muzzle of the .45 was inches away from, and aimed at! the center of his wife's forehead.

Tara stood there, lovely mouth agape, her green eyes wide, holding her breath in astonishment.

He sighed mightily, flicked on the safety and returned the .45 to its shoulder holster. "Now there was a real temptation." He returned back to the material spread out across the desk, "I thought we were going to avoid personal contact, Miss Carpenter. She crossed the hooch to stand behind him, resting a hand on his shoulder.

Her touch had always had its intended effect on him, he realized anew, whether it was intended to comfort, arouse or merely share, and now was no exception. He felt that humanizing affirmation borne of the touch of woman, of grace and beauty so uncommon in the harshness of war.

She glimpsed the paperwork heed been pouring over: three personnel files, a pad of his notations and the slim leather volume, folded open with the spine up. She read aloud the names off the personnel files.

"Captain Larson, Lieutenant Grey, Sergeant Hines. Primary suspects. Motives and opportunities galore. But I don't understand your interest in Sergeant Williams diary. 1m glad I don't have to guess which one of those three fragged the Colonel."

McCall decided that he could either blow Up or give up. He turned around to look up at her from where he sat and his exasperation yielded to affection in spite of himself. More than anyone, he could appreciate that this woman he was in love with had a backbone of steel coupled with a tenacity that could wear down stone.

"What makes you think I'm guessing? What I do is called investigating and detecting." He sighed again, allowing himself a chuckle. "What the hell am I going to do with you?"

An impish smile curved her lips and with one graceful, impudent motion! she was straddling his lap, her wrists lacked behind his neck! her mischievous green eyes aroused, her glistening, inviting lips only inches away.

She whispered huskily in his ear. "I've got an idea what you could do about it, Major."

"You vexatious wench."

"Vexatious?"

"Sometimes I wish you were more of a nag. That'd be easier to deal with."

Realizing that he was serious, she lost some of her good humor. "What about that diary? Was it interesting?"

"What diary?"

At that instant, someone outside yelled, *"Incoming!"*

Then everything was drowned out by a startling, eerie whistling that increased in pitch unbelievably fast and was then itself drowned out by a deafening explosion, an impacting blast that shook the hooch. Dust and red dirt powdered down upon them.

McCall grabbed the M-16 he'd been issued and hurried to the doorway.

A night fog had fallen. A bursting flare overhead cast the base in surreal daylight, as if seen through a mist.

The first explosion had been a direct hit on the Huey gunship that had brought them! now nothing but an unrecognizable, flaming ruin. Everywhere, soldiers were deploying! some firing their Ml6's on the run. He heard the steady, throaty hammering of the M-50's. There was Continuous incoming fire! winking saffron flickers in the night. He cursed when he saw a G.I. drop- Artillery and the morTara opened up returning fire shredding the night with their thunder and fury. The ground shook.

A round whistled in, chipping off a chunk of the hooch doorframe. McCall felt a trickle of blood from a flying splinter, razor-thin along his cheek. He absently wiped the blood away.

The next incoming mortar shell struck the main bunker. The Tactical Operations Command evaporated in a copper-red eruption of flame.

Tara was at his side, ready to bolt. "Damn but I wish they'd issued me a weapon. Don't suppose I could borrow one of yours?"

He grabbed her hand. "First let's get you to cover. They're targeting the hooches.

He yanked her with him and they stormed out into the battle. He led her to a nearby pile of debris, empty oil drums and discarded machine parts; a good place to stash a troublesome wife until this was over, They passed more Strobe- like explosions. Shouts filled the air along with the stench o destruction! of burnt gunpowder of dying and killing.

A round pinged off an overhanging piece of metal Tara's right, McCall reasoned. He couldn't leave her unarmed. He handed her his M-16, which left him with the shoulder- holstered .45.

"Here. You qualified with one of these on the range back home. Consider this a lesson in practical application. Keep your head down, babe. You are a non-combatant." He unleathered the .45 and flicked off the safety. "I got to keep moving, to help out."

She took the rifle, wholly comfortable with it. But her eyes were distracted by something behind him.

"Cord. Look"

He whirled, not knowing what to expect. Then he saw it

Through the disorganized melee, a soldier, whose features were obscured, became centralized in his focus for the same reason Tara had noticed him. Though he fit in, moving through the tumultuous fire-fight with determined haste, staying low to avoid incoming fire one hand steadying his helmet as he ran, he did appear to McCall even from this distance, to be somehow disengaged from the fighting, particularly when he reached the hooch that the McCalls had just vacated.

A shell-burst, much too close for comfort, clearly revealed the man's features in flickering, harsh coppery tones just before he entered the hooch.

"Dam," said Tara.

"Wait here," said McCall, and he bolted away from there.

Tara slung the M-16 over her shoulder by its strap as if she were a seasoned vet. She clicked her camera's flash bulb attachment into place.

"Right," she said to herself.

McCall hesitated at the entrance to the hooch, the .45 at his side, his presence undetected by the man inside because of the ferocious battle raging around them and because the man was preoccupied, in the process of reaching for the slim black book next to the files on the desk.

McCall said, "It's not a journal, Captain."

Larson whirled. His flinty eyes struggled between surprise and panic. "Major, I can explain."

They were shouting to be heard above the cacophony from outside.

I'm arresting you," shouted McCall. "You fragged the Colonel."

Larson drew himself up straight, doing his best to reassert command here even if he was outranked. On the strength of what? Every man on this base wanted that bastard dead."

"Yeah but I smoked out someone with a guilty conscience." McCall nodded to the black book. "That's no journal. It's a notebook I always carry. You wanted a look at it to see if you were incriminated. Williams told you to bite your tongue and take orders when you confided in him that you wanted to frag the Colonel

A shell struck the next hooch over with the thunderous crack! of a lightening strike. The ground whumped with its impact. Screams for "Medic! Medic!" came from close enough to sound like they were inside this hooch.

Like a jolt of electricity, this ignited raw, bitter emotion chat spewed from Larson. "That's exactly what he told me! Let it alone, he said. Follow orders. Right, follow orders! And look what it got Williams and the men of Bravo Company. When he realized what he'd said, he roared like a gored bull. *"Bastard!"*

He lunged at McCall.

McCall had hoped that sight of the .45 would discourage this, but Larson wasn't about to be taken easily. He could escape into the jungle! or die trying. McCall brought up the .45-

The snap! of a flashbulb came from close behind his ear.

Tara had crept up from outside, eavesdropping on everything. The flash tilled the hooch, not impairing McCall's vision because it came from behind him. But the blinding flash startled, stunned and stopped Larson, who reflexively threw his arms up to cover his eyes.

McCall heard Tara say, "Gotcha!"

He charged the disoriented man, bringing his pistol around in a swipe that cracked the side of Larson's head. Larson's knees buckled. He collapsed to the earthen floor. McCall holstered his .45 and reached for his cuffs, speaking over his shoulder to Tara who, camera still in hand, looked stunning in her form-fitting fatigues even with the beauty of her model's face grime-smudged and her red hair tangled.

"Thanks, hon" He looked down at Larson, whose face, against the earthen floor, was an emotionless mask. "You must have radioed in for air cover as soon as this attack started. We'll hitch a ride back to Saigon when it's over."

"You've got this all wrong, Major. Yeah, I thought it was a journal. I came to see if the sarge thought anyone on base would do it, sce if ha wrote it down. That doesn't mean I fragged him!"

"Hines will fess up," said McCall. "He's lying to give you an alibi because he hated the coloncl too. You weren't in the TOC bunker with Hines when the Colonel was fragged. I'll go to work on Top's conscience and his duty under the Uniform Code of Military Justice, and when your First Sergeant talks, I have the proof I need."

"What the hell kind of a soldier are you?" sneered Larson. "Whose side are you on, McCall? I'm on the side of our soldiers. That's more important than any VC body count, so some fat-assed Colonel can advance his career. You think I could let that go on? Our body count is my concern!" He cooled, his tone reasonable. "Let me go, Major. The Colonel got what he deserved. You know that, in your heart."

"Sorry, Captain. It's my lob to take you in."

Someone outside yelled, *"Incoming!"* and again came that fast-approaching whistling.

McCall sprang at Tara without hesitation, yelling to the man upon the floor, "Move it, Cap! Save yourself!

Larson didn't move. He said in a calm voice, "Up yours, Major."

With the incoming whistle louder with every heartbeat, McCall plowed into Tara with enough force to knock her off her feet, sending them both airborne pitching them outside and to ground. They landed together, his arms encircling her. They rolled a few times and came to a stop.

A direct hit demolished the hooch with another loud explosion.

McCall pinned his wife almost as he had on the cot but this time to shield her. They were pelted with falling debris. When the shower ceased, they lifted their heads.

She arched her neck for a view of the smoldering remains of the hooch. "Captain Larson...!!"

"It better this way," said McCall. "He died a combatant. It will look better in his file."

"You're not going to report that he killed the Colonel?"

McCall said nothing.

She stared up at him. Then she kissed the thin red line of dried blood that crossed his cheek.

The battle was winding down. Three Huey gunships rotored in and began pulverizing the jungle, making the night sky a fire show of tracer bullets, rocket fire and multiple explosions from inside the tree line. The M-6G's on the perimeter, and the base morTara and artillery, stayed at it.

There was no more incoming fire. The primary activity on the base was centered on tending the wounded, regrouping, assessing the damage.

And for one stolen moment between a man and a woman, upon the battle-scarred ground of Firebase Tiger, McCall and his wife prolonged their embrace that would appear to any passerby as no more than a soldier shielding a noncombatant after that last explosion.

"Know what?' whispered Tara.

"What?

"I like being on the bottom

"You," McCall said," are impossible."

"And that's only one of the reasons you're crazy about me, right?!!

"Yeah, I guess so," McCall admitted. "Crazy is definitely the word. I must be out of my mind, He saw two figures hurrying in their direction. "Here comes Sergeant Hines and Lieutenant Grey. I've got some explaining to do." He got up off of her, extending a courtly hand. She accepted, rising to her feet. He said for her ears alone, "Now stow the personal stuff, okay, hon? I mean it, Tara. For real."

He turned to greet Hines and the Lieutenant,

"Right," Tara said to herself, and hurried to join them.

III

CHEZ EROTIQUE: A MCCALL
& TARA MYSTERY

CHEZ EROTIQUE

TARA WANTED to try a new position from the *Kama Sutra*.

After thirty minutes, though, the sexual heat between her and McCall built to such sweat-drenched, panting intensity that they decided the hell with the *Kama Sutra* and switched to that good old, wonderfully serviceable missionary position.

Cord McCall was dark-haired and well muscled. He tossed Tara onto her back, enthusiastically shifting her from the convoluted position in which they had been finding panting bliss. Tara guided his hardness into her, to the hilt.

The woman who was calling herself Tara Carpenter was seven years Cord's junior. Her hair was red. Her eyes were green, attentive and mischievous. Her body was firm and perfectly proportioned. She wrapped her legs around him and gasped happily when their hips melded and began driving together. Her face was flushed, her Irish eyes dancing with hunger, not satisfaction.

McCall clasped her petite behind, and the feverish, almost desperate coupling took on the rhythms and the ways he knew she liked, generating mutual, intensifying fires stoked with every delicious thrust.

BEDSPRINGS ROCKED. Sheets became hot and tangled.

Tara kissed him madly. "Oh God, Cord. *Yes!*"

That's when the telephone rang.

McCall's hips ceased their pistoning. His erection began to subside. He gave her bottom a loving squeeze and released it.

"Sorry, hon."

He eased from her.

Major McCall was an investigator assigned to a special operations unit of the Joint Criminal Investigation Division detachment. He was off-duty, and they were in the bedroom of his private living quarters.

Tara reluctantly allowed her ankles to unlock, and her legs to loosen their hold on him.

"CORD, sweetie, it's two o'clock in the morning," she pouted. Tara wasn't the pouting type, but right now it gave her a sultry look. "Can't you--"

He shook his head, lifting the receiver while positioned between her legs.

"This time of day is when my work happens." Into the mouthpiece of the phone he said, curtly, "McCall."

A male voice said, without preamble, "I am sorry to bother you, Major." The caller spoke precise English with a Viet accent.

McCall grunted, recognizing the voice. "Not as sorry as I am, Major. What's up?"

Major Ngu Pham was McCall's counterpart, an investigator for the Army of the Republic of Vietnam's criminal investigation division. McCall and Pham had worked cases together when US military and ARVN interests were jointly concerned in an investigation. Pham had proven himself to be a man of intelligence, wit, integrity, and honesty.

Of COURSE, honesty was a relative term these days in Saigon, with plenty of gray area. Pham was exemplary at performing his investigative duties when they worked together, and so McCall had allowed himself to be nonjudgmental when he learned that the dapper, good-natured ARVN officer also happened to be part owner of an exclusive sex club, *Chez Erotique*, in the city's red light district.

McCall and Pham were presently involved in an undercover probe, a joint effort to take down a robust black market operation.

Pham said, "I apologize for calling you at this hour, Major, but we have a problem. Both of us."

McCall disengaged from Tara, wrapping an arm around her to draw her to him as he stretched out on his back.

"Are we talking about Mr. Smith?"

"Frankly," said Pham, "as a friend and colleague, I am hoping that you will be the one to determine that."

"Mr. Smith," which everyone understood to be a cover name, was said to be the primary shaper and mover of the lucrative black market underground operating in Saigon. But Mr. Smith was more an elusive presence than a person, it seemed. One word from Mr. Smith and people died, and yet no one appeared to know the identity of this mysterious figure.

"Okay," said McCall, "let's hear it."

"Sergeant Samuels is dead."

McCall grunted. "Then it's got something to do with Mr. Smith."

"Yes, you've told me; he was your undercover operative."

"Informant," McCall corrected.

"He told you today that tonight he would learn the identity of Mr. Smith." Pham paused. "Uh, Major, I regret to inform you that the sergeant was murdered tonight at *Chez Erotique*. I'm there now. I've just arrived. Since we have combined our efforts to investigate Mr. Smith, I thought it best to call you first."

McCall became aware of Tara's fingers stroking his flaccid member. As he started to throb, he forced himself to keep focused on the conversation. He sent Tara a reproving glance and brushed her fingers away, wishing like hell that he didn't have to.

"You thought right," he told Pham. "Okay, you owe me one. Get out of there. Our investigation is undercover. Let's keep it that way for a few more hours."

"That would be beneficial."

"This conversation isn't taking place," said McCall. "You aren't there tonight."

"I see. I understand."

"I'm on my way down there," said McCall. "An American soldier has been murdered, and I'm investigating. I'll find out what happened, and I'll take care of it. You're not involved."

"THANK YOU, Major. You're right. I do owe you one, as you say. The woman who manages this establishment for me, the Madame, her name is Tran Le. I trust her."

And the phone connection went dead.

McCall swung his bare feet to the floor as he replaced the receiver. He reached for a casual shirt and jeans on a nearby chair.

Tara left the bed, a vision of curvy perfection.

"Where to, Major?"

McCall slipped into his shoulder holster to accommodate an Army issue Colt. 45 automatic that he habitually carried under his left arm, concealed by a lightweight sports jacket.

"Where do you think? I'm taking you home. I've got work to do."

She emerged from the bathroom less than two minutes later.

The lust had left her eyes, but not the mischievous glint. "So we've got another case?"

"I SAID I'm taking you home, Tara."

They left his quarters together.

Although nobody in Vietnam, or anywhere else, was aware of it, he and Tara were husband and wife.

Tara was a professional news photographer back in "the world." By assuming a last-name change and hoodwinking her news media employers stateside, and the military, she'd scammed an assignment to cover the duties of a certain CID investigator in Saigon.

Posing as Tara Carpenter, Mrs. Cord McCall was after nothing less a Pulitzer Prize, a new, woman's slant on the war. And, she'd explained to her initially astonished husband upon her arrival in Vietnam, she wanted to experience his world. He had reluctantly agreed to maintain the deception.

Because time was now of the absolute essence, he likewise relented now and allowed Tara to accompany him on the drive from the base, into the heart of Saigon.

Except for occasional urban guerrilla actions by the Vietcong, life in Saigon was largely unscathed by the direct violence of the war. The streets were raucous even now, in the middle of the night, clogged with cars, trucks, trishaws, pedicabs and many bicycles. Itinerate vendors wandered in hordes, shrilly hawking their wares.

As HIS '67 Pontiac negotiated this maze, McCall told her about the call that had interrupted their lovemaking. He told her about Major Pham, about what a good investigator Pham was, and about the ARVN officer's part ownership of a sex club.

Tara had seen her share of the realities of life before and after meeting McCall, and she listened without comment.

"I busted Sergeant Samuels just yesterday," he told her. "He was a rotten soldier, a disgrace to the uniform. He was diverting merchandise from the Post Exchange, the enlisted man's club and the officers club, raking in a profit selling everything from nylons to beer to transistor radios to food on the black market, for top dollar to Viet civilians. He roughed up a bookkeeper at the PX who wouldn't look the other way, and the bookkeeper came to CID. I busted him, but I after I let him sweat awhile, I let him go."

Tara nodded. "You still want to bust the Vietnamese end of the operation. And tonight the sergeant is dead in a swanky sex club. Coincidence?"

"Don't believe in 'em," said McCall. "The sarge got so close to Mr. Smith, and he got himself dead. When I find who stuck a knife into Sergeant Samuels, I'll have Mr. Smith."

"*We* will have him, darling," she said sweetly.

McCall concentrated on his driving.

He had more than once regretted his decision to be part of her deception, but there were those occasions when Tara had, in fact, supplied an interpretation or observation that had helped him solve a case...

THE LITTLE TEXAS red light district of Saigon was a densely cluttered sprawl near the harbor, adjacent to Duong Tu-Do, Liberty Street, the busy boulevard that bisected the nation's capital; a neon-and-rabble full world of civilians, troops, gangsters, deserters, refugees and black marketeers.

PROSTITUTES, who were everywhere, dressed in the exaggerated, garish sexuality of their profession, calling out to every male in sight.

Chez Erotique was a three-story brick structure, set back from the street, the ornate ironwork around its windows an elegant holdover from the days of French colonialism.

This was a sedate, upscale bordello, a world apart from the gaudy neon fleshpots surrounding it. This was where gentlemen from the American and Viet military and private sectors could, if they were able to meet the price, pay for their kinky pleasures and discreetly indulge them with, it was said, the prettiest "working girls" in Saigon. This wasn't a bump-and-grind sweathouse for over-heated infantrymen. This was class for those who could afford it, priced to keep out the riff-raff.

The interior of the house was comfortably air-conditioned, designed to lull and appeal to the senses. Muted traditional Vietnamese music wafted through the air, as did the scent of lavender incense. The furnishings were plush, with a lot of pillows, and the lighting was soft, indirect.

In a second-floor bedroom, the corpse of Sergeant Samuels was sprawled out upon its chest, across the rumpled sheets of an antique iron bed.

Despite the incense, the walls of the room seemed to emanate a musky, cloying aura of sex, as if these walls had absorbed the essence over the years of the endless carnal activity that went on in here.

Beyond one wall, in the next room, rocking bedsprings and enthusiastic lovemaking could be heard faintly.

The dead man was a Caucasian, with a military buzz cut. His slacks and shorts were gathered around his knees, and a knife had been rammed to the hilt into his lower back, beneath the bottom left rib.

TARA AND TRAN LE, the Madame, stood near the closed

doorway behind McCall, watching him lean forward to examine the body.

Tara said, "I don't suppose this place is any stranger to the Little Death, as our French friends like to call the orgasm. But I'm curious, Tran Le." She indicated the corpse. "Is this is a first?"

The Madame nodded. "*Oui. Le petite morte.* It is the reason *Chez Erotique* exists." Tran Le was Eurasian, close to thirty; too old to be one of a working girl here, but embodying a ripened maturity that McCall had always found alluring. Her jet-black hair was pinned up elegantly. A gown that revealed everything, yet nothing of curvaceous body accentuated her allure. Her hands and arms were draped with a shawl of pale blue silk. She nodded at the dead man. "I am happy to say that this is the first time an American, or anyone else, has ever befallen such misfortune at *Chez Erotique.*" She spoke in a throaty voice, with a French accent. "As a matter of fact," she added, "we pride ourselves on our security measures."

"He wasn't supposed to be here," said McCall. "This place is off limits to American personnel."

Tran Le raised one eyebrow and shrugged an aristocratic, worldly smile. "Men are wont to go wherever they wish, when they wish, regardless of rules and regulations, is that not so, Major?"

Tara hadn't missed McCall's admiring visual inventory of Tran Le. She cleared her throat.

"Has he been dead long?" she asked. There was a trace of cattiness in her tone.

UNDERSTANDABLE, McCall reasoned. After all, what wife wants her husband checking out another woman, right in front of her?

"I'm no medical examiner," he said, "and I'd like to remind you, Miss Carpenter, that your job is to photograph me at work, not help me solve the cases."

Tran Le eyed Tara solely for the first time.

"Photograph?" Her smooth forehead creased with a frown. "But there can be no photographs. I run a very discreet operation here, you see."

"DON'T WORRY, HON," said Tara, "there won't be any photographs. I was visiting the Major when you called." She placed a minor emphasis on the word visiting, suggestive enough for Tran Le to get the message.

Great, thought McCall. I'm dealing with a homicide, and the wife decides to get jealous in a whorehouse.

Tran Le addressed McCall. "The dead man is an American soldier. I searched his wallet when I first stepped in here. His name is Tom Samuels. He's a sergeant. He was in this room with one of my girls. She ran to me after the attack."

"WAS THE SERGEANT A REGULAR PATRON HERE?" he asked.

She sniffed. "Most certainly not. Monetary considerations of the average enlisted man generally preclude their patronage of *Chez Erotique.* I have never seen this man before." She clasped the sleeve of his jacket. "Major, Ngu Pham said that you would help. That you would act in our best interests." She indicated the body. "Can this be somehow kept from an official report, at least insofar as it having happened here?

"How quiet has this been so far?"

"As I say, the girl came directly to me," said Tran Le. "I came in here to see for myself. I searched his wallet for identification. I called Major Pham, and he came here and called you before he left."

The lovemaking in the next room intensified.

Tara said, "Is the girl who found the body as cool-headed about it as you are?"

"She is a good girl," Tran Le said in a neutral voice. "A woman sees many things in our line of work, my dear. And I would not be so hostile toward me if I were you. Circumstance and chance have been less kind to me than to you, perhaps. But in any event, I supply only what is sought."

"IN OTHER WORDS, KITTEN," said McCall to Tara, "pull in your claws."

Tara started to respond angrily, then paused, then visibly relaxed.

"I'm sorry, Tran Le," she said in a subdued voice. "Your points are well taken." She swung her eyes back to McCall. "But don't you have a duty to call this into the authorities or something?"

"I AM THE AUTHORITIES," he reminded her. "Pardon the bad grammar. But we have an inside track here. Let's see where it takes us." He looked back at the body. Some blood had seeped from around the knife and was partly congealed on the sheet beneath to the body. "The blade pierced his heart. He must have died instantly."

Tara hugged herself, shivering. "What a terrible experience for the girl he was with."

"You will help me, Major?" asked Tran Le, "to, uh, clear this up, is that the saying?"

"That's it," said McCall. "I don't know yet what happened here, but I am going to find out who killed this man."

"That would be the thing to do," nodded Tara wryly. "I mean, you being a homicide investigator and all."

McCall tried to ignore her.

He asked Tran Le, "So no one knows about this yet except you and the girl who found the body?"

"That is correct."

"Did she describe the killer to you? She'd get a look at him if she was on the bottom."

"SHE TOLD me that the sergeant wanted the room dark. She claims to have seen nothing."

"Tran Le, have you ever heard the name Mr. Smith?"

She studied him uncertainly. "Is that a joke, Major? Is that not a common American name, and one often used in an establishment such as this?"

"Yeah, I suppose it is," said McCall. "Okay, no Mr. Smith. I need to talk to the girl who found the body."

Tran Le's smile was uncomfortable, contrite. "I regret to say that after Major Pham left here, there were complications."

McCall frowned. "What sort of complications?"

"The prostitute who was with the sergeant was hysterical, as I've said. I'm afraid she'd gone."

McCall's frown deepened. "Gone?"

"She was left unattended but for an instant, but she ran screaming into the night. I have taken steps to see that she is returned."

"What kind of steps?"

"My security manager--"

"You mean, your bouncer," McCall interjected.

Tran Le's bosom moved with a sigh beneath her pale shawl. "As you like. His name is Ky. He is a most formidable man in these matters, and he knows every inch of Little Texas. I have sent him after her. She will not escape from Ky for long. He will return here with her."

"Has Major Pham been told of this?"

"He has. He asked you to allow Ky thirty minutes to find and return with the girl. He begs your indulgence."

Tara was studying McCall. "Your ARVN friend

seems to have plenty of that, doesn't he, Major? Your indulgence, I mean."

"A good man in the ARVN CID is a good connection to have," McCall growled. "The only thing I want is to solve this murder." He glanced at the sergeant's bare-assed body, trousers, and underwear tangled around its knees. "But I respect Major Pham enough to play this his way for thirty minutes. No," he snapped at Tran Le, "make that fifteen. Your man has fifteen minutes to turn up this girl. I need to question her."

"BUT OF COURSE, MAJOR." Tran Le's eyes shone with gratitude. "And during those fifteen minutes, perhaps you and the lady," she nodded to Tara, "would care to relax here at Chez Erotique. Many couples avail themselves of our facilities; you may be surprised to learn."

"AND HOW," asked Tara, "would a couple indulge themselves here during a fifteen minute wait?"

The Madame smiled. "I would suggest one of our private shows. Couples or singles may watch erotic performances from their personal, private booth." She glanced at the watch on her slim brown wrist. "A show is about to begin. Would you care to observe?"

McCall couldn't pull his eyes from the sight of the dead man on the bed.

"Seems like a hell of a way to conduct a murder

investigation. That hysterical prostitute could be a prime suspect."

Tara playfully slapped McCall's arm. Her green eyes glinted.

"Major, waiting is waiting. And we haven't seen a good sex show in, oh, what's it been now, at least an hour?"

McCall bristled. "Miss Campbell--" he started to say.

"But of course," Tran Le said, taking Tara by the arm in a friendly, familiar fashion and adroitly guiding her out of the room.

WHEN THEY WERE GONE, McCall paused. He crossed the room and removed a sheet from the bed. He spread the cloth across the body then left the room, stepping into the corridor, closing the door behind him.

THE HALLWAY RAN the length of the building and was lined with doors to private rooms along either side.

HE STRODE past some men moving with women toward separate rooms. One guy had two girls with him. The prostitutes McCall saw, up here on the second floor, were all Vietnamese, dressed pretty much alike in high heels that attractively jutted out the ass and breasts, shapely legs encased in colored thigh-high stockings, with tight waists and breasts encased in lace that accentuated deep cleavage. From behind doors, he heard exuberant lovemaking. From behind one, a man's gravelly voice, pleading, and a harsh feminine voice and the snap of a whip. From behind another, the sound of women making love.

Tran Le had paused with Tara next to a curtained doorway at the far end of the hallway. The two women were getting along famously, chatting in discreet, lowered voices with the occasional smile, while the scents and sounds of lovemaking permeated the surroundings.

When McCall joined them, Tara said, with that mischievous glint in her eye, "Tran Le was telling me about what we're about to see."

The Madame flashed McCall a delicate smile. "I hope, Major, that you are not easily shocked."

"Not by sex," said McCall. "It's the other things people do to each other that get me upset."

"Of course, I understand. Your reason for being here is the murder of an American soldier. I thank you for your patience, truly. I personally assure you that my man will have found the girl and brought her back here before this performance is concluded. This way, please, if you please."

McCall decided, *Ah, what the hell.*

They stepped beyond the curtain, into a narrow hall that led off the main corridor and curved sharply to the left where it widened to a series of closed doors.

TRAN LE OPENED the nearest door and they stepped into an extremely compact room--more of a booth--that was dimly lighted, carpeted, furnished with a single plush couch that faced a window that comprised a quarter of one wall. Beyond the glass, a room was lighted in soft pink hues. There was no furniture out there, only a small dais and a row of opaque windows, matching the one of this booth, lining the walls facing the dais.

"One-way glass," McCall observed.

"We guarantee our patrons absolute privacy to engage in whatever pleasures they wish," said Tran Le. "Is there anything else I can do for you?"

"No thanks," said Tara. "We'll just pretend we're customers for a little while, right, Major?"

McCall grumbled. "Customers trying to solve a murder."

"If you'll excuse me," said Tran Le.

With a nod to each of them, she let herself out.

As soon as the door latched behind her, McCall stepped to it and tried the handle. It opened. He closed it, fighting the urge to unholster his .45 and flick off its safety.

Tara eyed his every move, intuitively reading him as she always did.

"I know, Cord. But I don't think that being brought back here is a trap. Whoever killed the sergeant is long gone by now, don't you think?"

McCall turned from the door and slipped an arm around his wife's trim waist, yanking her to him. She emitted a surprised gasp of pleasure as he began nuzzling her left ear.

"Oh, Major."

"I'm thinking this room may be bugged," he whispered.

Her hands clasped behind at his neck and she purred happily.

She whispered into his ear, "I hope Tran Le isn't your killer. I like her. I like people who put me in my place."

"I'd like to put you on a plane back to the States," he growled irritably. "I must have been out of my mind from the start, going along with this nutty charade of yours."

"We're both crazy, darling. Happily, about each other. But let's talk about the sergeant. And your friend, Major Pham. Exactly how much do you trust him, Cord? Could he be Mr. Smith?"

McCall sighed. *This woman*, he thought. Tara's tenacity was a force of nature. It was one of the things he loved about her. He also loved the way her firm, shapely figure felt in his arms. The fragrance of her tingled his senses.

The fact that this was a bogus clinch, intended to allow him to communicate with her in case the booth was bugged, did not diminish the warm urgency of her firm breasts and hips pressing against him. Their loving had gone uncompleted when they were interrupted by Tran Le's phone call and now, with Tara in his arms, the sexual tension was returning. McCall found himself growing hard in his slacks. His hardness surged against the thin layers of fabric that separated them.

"Look," said McCall. He rotated her around in his arms without releasing his embrace, so they could both watch through the one-way window. "Show's about to start."

The lilting Vietnamese music faded, replaced by subtle American jazz with a strong bass line and backbeat.

In syncopation to this beat, two dancers--one male, one female--approached the dais from opposite sides of the room beyond the glass.

The man was muscular and taller than the average Vietnamese with a well-developed physique, clad only in a skimpy thong loincloth.

The woman embodied the beauty of Vietnamese womanhood. Slim, with a muscular litheness to her tawny thighs and shoulders. Her black hair was stylishly short, framing a lovely face dominated by lush lips and sensual eyes. She wore high heels and white nylons. Her curvy hips were encased in a bikini bottom. Above that she wore only a smile and a shawl, identical to the one worn by Tran Le except that the Madame's patterned shawl had been pale in color, while the dancer's shawl and its oriental pattern were bright, shimmering in the tasteful lighting.

A light fog swirled in from an unseen smoke

machine, licking the floor and walls, lending the artfully lighted dais a dream-like quality.

The dancers faced each other, swaying. The woman's shoulders shimmied gently, gracefully, their feminine roundness accentuated by the artfully draped shawl. The dancers turned from each other to face Tara and Cord, and the others in the other enclosures.

McCall could only guess at what was happening behind those windows.

The dancers undulated, eyes closed, erotically caressing themselves in intimate places and ways to the beat of the music. They turned again to each other and moved into a steamy embrace, their lips meeting in an extended kiss. One of the man's hands slid beneath the shawl to cup an unseen breast, and palm it. She leaned her head back, eyes closed, and mouthed a silent, extended moan.

The pulse of the music intensified.

In the booth, as McCall stood there his arms around Tara, both of them watching the performance, he became aware of the subtle twitch and steady grinding of his wife's butt against the front of his slacks. Tara slid her hands down to clasp each of his hands. She guided his hands, one to her left breast, the other to the front of her skirt. He felt her sexual hunger pulsating through the denim.

She squeezed each of his hands tightly to her with her hot fingers and continued moving her hips, her eyes glued to the embracing dancers beyond the glass.

"OH BABY," Tara moaned. "Uh, guess I'm still, uh, horny because we didn't finish at your place..."

On the dais, the male tightened his embrace. The woman swayed and the shawl dropped to form a luminous pool at her feet. He lowered his lips, began to kiss and fondle her milky white breasts topped with taut brown nipples.

There was suddenly no air conditioning in the booth. There was only heat, humidity and the sweet scent of arousal.

Tara's shapely behind continued its rotation against the front of his slacks, deliciously caressing his growing erection.

Curls of artificial smoke partially obscured the entwined couple on the dais. The man danced behind the woman, holding her possessively. He was visually aroused. He drew her to him, and she obeyed willingly. Their dance was less than coitus, more than suggestive.

But as McCall held his undulating wife, much as the male beyond the glass held the woman, McCall found himself unable to stop looking at the luminous pool of the dancer's discarded shawl on the dais. Something, elusive at first in his subconscious, was calling to be heard. And then his conscious mind got it. His erection shrunk as the thought process raced through his mind.

Tara noticed his erection subside. She turned in his arms to face him. But for her somewhat flustered look, you could hardly tell that she'd just been interrupted in the throes of sexual passion.

"HONEY, WHAT IS IT?"

"Beautiful, this is going to have to wait. The time for fun is after the work is done. I just thought of something."

Reality was intruding on the heat that had consumed her for a mad moment.

She sighed. "Sorry, honey. I guess I'll always be bad in the self-discipline department."

"You're not much good for mine, either," he muttered. He was already turning to swing the door inward, striding out of the booth. "That's why I don't like having you around."

She hurried to keep up with him.

In the main corridor, there was presently no one in sight, although voices carried up to the second-floor landing from downstairs.

MCCALL STALKED off to the landing and down the stairs. Tara stayed with him. They met a man coming up the stairs.

The Viet civilian was stocky, wearing creased slacks, a Hawaiian shirt and a pistol holstered at his hip that identified him as the house security man, most likely ARVN or police, thought McCall. His job would be to sit in the foyer where he would be seen by newly arriving patrons, a reminder to enjoy themselves but to not cause trouble.

"I am Ky," he announced brusquely. "You are Major McCall?"

McCall nodded. "Did you find the girl?"

Ky turned, leading them downstairs. "Tran Le sent me to get you. I have just returned."

At the bottom of the stairs, he led them across the foyer to double doors that were opposite the main parlor--dimly lighted, furnished with a bar and over-stuffed couches--where half a dozen young ladies mingled with an equal number of men.

Ky led them through the swing doors. McCall was close on his heels, his fingertips near the butt of the concealed .45. Tara was right behind McCall.

It was a woman's lounge, a place where the girls of *Chez Erotique* could freshen up. To one side was a half-open door leading to a row of stalls facing a row of sinks and mirrors; to the other, a tiled communal shower.

In this connecting room, Tran Le was engaged in an animated, overheated conversation in Vietnamese with one of her prostitutes who looked to be no more than a teenager despite the rouge, heels, camisole, and the other would-be trappings of adulthood.

Tran Le held onto each of her wrists, her tone alternating argumentatively between stern recrimination and persuasion. The girl was resisting but not really struggling, obviously intimidated.

Ky sidled from McCall's side to stand near a wall, hovering there with his eyes on Tran Le. He reminded McCall of a wrestler waiting for his signal to join in a tag team match.

Tara remained close to McCall's other side.

Tran Le released the girl.

"Major, I'm so glad you're here." She rearranged the pale shawl that was in disarray around her hands and arms; the shawl with the Asian print that again reminded McCall of the brighter, otherwise identical shawl worn by the dancer. Tran Le nodded to the disheveled prostitute who was cowering in a corner. "As you can see, my man has retrieved the girl." The Madame spoke coolly. "She denies killing your soldier, of course, but I can see where no one else would have the motive or the opportunity. This misguided child killed him for his wallet, of course, and then panicked. Murder is not for everyone."

The prostitute wailed from where she clung piti- fully to her corner of the room. "I no kill anyone! I good fuck girl! Sergeant, he fuck me. Lights go out. Someone attack sergeant. Everything happen! Then quiet. I turn light on and sergeant, he dead. Killer gone. I good fuck girl! I no killer!"

McCall stepped forward and took the girl gently by each of her elbows. She cringed from him at first, until she realized that he was guiding her to Tara, who saw something in his expression that prompted her to place an arm around the girl.

McCall turned to Tran Le.

"The dancer in that peep show you steered us to was wearing a shawl exactly like yours. Same print and everything. Except for one thing. Yours is pale. Hers was bright. That kept bugged me, down in my subcon- scious. I don't know why. But I just know got it. Your shawl is exactly like that dancer's, except you're wearing yours inside out. That started me wondering why."

He stepped toward Tran Le.

She stepped back. "Stay away from me, Major."

He reached out and snatched the shawl from about her before she could react. He held up the shawl.

Smeared blood on its inverse side was clearly visible.

"You were concealing these bloodstains that you picked up when you turned off the lights in that bedroom and stuck a knife into the sergeant's back. You couldn't get rid of the shawl, I guess. It must be part of your standard apparel and you didn't want to draw attention to yourself. So you simply wore it inside out, to conceal the bloodstains."

She drew herself erect, her aristocratic features haughty and aloof.

"That is quite ridiculous. One of the girls injured herself yesterday. That is how the bloodstain--"

"Stop it," said McCall. "You killed the sergeant, Tran Le."

Tara was frowning. "But Cord, why did she kill Sergeant Samuels?"

Tran Le scrutinized him with an arched eyebrow. "Yes, Major." Her words dripped venom. "What was my motive?"

"The only motive that would justify you murdering him, Tran Le, is that he pegged *you* as Mr. Smith. He told me he was closing in, and he came here. Major

Pham isn't involved, or he wouldn't have been asked me to come here in the first place. Instead of coming to me with the information like he was supposed to, the sergeant tried to sell you his silence. That's the kind of weasel he was, and that was real stupid of him because you shut him up permanently. You could have had your enforcer here, Ky, do the killing, but those bloodstains tell me that this was important enough for you to want to deal with it yourself, and you did."

Ky sneered where he remained near a wall. "American, you talk shit. Where is your proof?"

"Forensics will match up the stains on Tran Le's shawl with the sergeant's blood," said McCall. "And that, dragon lady, is the end for you. You should've stayed with the black market and left murder alone."

Tran Le hissed like an angry snake. There was a flash of tanned, perfectly shaped thigh with a garter that held a folded knife matching the knife handle that had protruded from the sergeant back. This knife seemed to leap into her hand, and a flick of her wrist made the blade snap open.

"Ky!" she snarled.

They came at McCall from both sides at once. Tran Le lunged for his throat with the skill of a street fighter. Ky plunged in, unholstering his pistol.

McCall heard a startled gasp from Tara and a wail of despair from the prostitute.

HE SNAP-KICKED the knife from Tran Le's hand. It clattered to the tile floor. She hissed again and darted for the door.

McCALL COULD NOT GO after her because by then Ky was practically on him, his pistol drawn.

Tara threw herself past him, after Tran Le.

McCall brought his .45 from the concealed shoulder rig in a lightning fast cross-draw, swinging the automatic outward in a wide, stiff-armed arc that smacked Ky sharply upside his head with the barrel.

Ky toppled to the floor, unconscious.

Tara tackled Tran Le in a flying dive, and they both went to the floor just short of the door.

McCall briskly stepped over there, holstering the .45. He produced stainless steel handcuffs from a pocket.

Tara rolled free.

McCall cuffed Tran Le's wrists behind her back before the Madame could regain her balance from Tara's tackle. McCall assisted Tran Le to her feet.

She didn't struggle, but she was swearing quietly, vehemently at McCall, alternating between sewer English, French and Vietnamese.

Tara led the girl prostitute to a couch.

The girl sank onto the couch. She looked like a frightened child in whore's clothing. "I work here." She jabbered in heavily accented English. "I good fuck girl." Her terrified flashed to Tran Le. "Men like! Why she say I murder sergeant? She know I not murder anybody! I good fuck girl! *Why?*" She broke down into uncontrollable sobbing.

Tara sat beside her on the couch, embracing the woman-child like an older sister, making cooing, comforting sounds that had a calming effect.

The girl lowered her face to Tara's shoulder. Her sobbing became more subdued.

"When I asked Tran Le about Mr. Smith," McCall said, "she decided to provide us with a fall guy. This girl was made to order."

Tara glared at Tran Le. "I've changed my mind, Cord. I don't like this bitch at all. And I guess I'm not much of a detective."

"No," he conceded, "but you are hell on wheels in a peep show, and there's something to be said for that."

Sitting there, caring for a young woman in need, dressed as she was not in showy high heels and pearls and camisole but in a sensible blouse and skirt, Tara remained, for McCall, the most appealing, arousing, sexiest woman he'd ever known.

Faces appeared in the doorway of the lounge, drawn by the scuffle. There was much alarm and murmuring when the Madame was seen in handcuffs. Then everyone scrambled. The doorway and the building quickly emptied.

TARA NOTED, "Looks like we've got the place to ourselves."

"Murder's always a good way to clear out a whore-house," said McCall.

He guided Tran Le to the doorway. She allowed herself to be led in sullen, brooding silence.

He said, "I'll find a phone and call the American MPs. If I call the Saigon cops of ARVN, the way this town is rigged, she'd be back out on the street in a week." He winked at his wife, for her eyes only. "I want this wrapped up and us back home, Miss Carpenter. You and I have some unfinished business."

Comforting the young prostitute, Tara flashed McCall a dazzling smile. "When it comes to you, Major, that's my favorite kind!"

IV

THE DARK OF MIDNIGHT

THE DARK OF MIDNIGHT

CHINA, 1939

THE HALF-TON FLATBED BARRELED through the main gate, ripping the gate from its hinges, tossing wood and wire aside and barreling on through.

Captain Midnight white-knuckled the steering wheel with his right hand. He extended his left arm through the open window of the truck and triggered a round from his .45 that caught a sentry in the chest and flung the man, wide-armed, back into the guardhouse.

"Hunch down below their line of fire, Chuck!"

Chuck Ramsey rode in the passenger seat with one hand on the dash and a palm against the windshield. His chin lifted, his eyes set with more than his usual degree of seventeen-year-old rebelliousness.

"Uh uh, Cap. You need two sets of eyes. Watch your ten o'clock!"

He saw what Chuck saw and tore off two more rounds, then concentrated on driving with both hands. The half-ton skidded into a two-wheeled turn. Tires left the pavement, then gained traction, spewing dirt before thundering down a narrow, winding road.

Dawn smudged a crimson streak across a steel gray horizon. Shadows cloaked the towering medieval castle behind them, a sprawling four-level edifice of winged, tiled roofs, balconies and turrets. A klaxon horn started wailing. A pair of sentries summoned the courage to leave their cover of the guardhouse and open fire. Angry hornets pierced the truck cab.

The majority of General Tong's ragtag force had been occupied feeding some poor devil to the hogs. Captain Midnight and Chuck had been on the fourth level of the massive castle, rifling through the general's safe, when the hideous screams first reached them, causing them to wince; an unholy cacophony, the shrieking, shrill squeals barely recognizable as human. The grunting of hogs feasting, snorting, dull teeth gnawing away chunks of living flesh from whoever had been staked out in the pen. And the cruel laughter. The death cries had subsided by the time the American duo rappelled down from a window, the plans for the bombsite in a side pocket of Captain Midnight's jacket. They commandeered the truck and escaped detection until the final bust-out.

Chuck twisted around, staring along the backtrack. "Dang, Cap! They're already on our tail!"

He saw it too in his rearview mirror. A pair of

trucks came bolting in pursuit, the beds top-heavy with men waving rifles. Another angry hornet drilled the windshield. Bullets spanged off the truck's chassis.

Captain Midnight shouted to be heard. "Chuck, take the wheel!" Chuck gripped the rollicking steering wheel with both hands. Captain Midnight eased open his door against the centrifugal force and steadied one boot on the running board. He unclipped a miniature device from his belt and tossed it into the cab. "Call in Joyce for the pickup." A bullet whistled between his body and the cab, shattering the outside rearview mirror.

Chuck drove with one hand while he thumbed the hand-held radio, an invention of Captain Midnight's alter ego, world-famous millionaire inventor James "Red" Albright.

"SQ-2 calling SQ-3. SQ-2 calling SQ-3. Would there by any chance be a beautiful blonde in the vicinity, looking for two easy pickups?"

Joyce Ryan's cool response carried crisply through the rumbling rattle and roll of the wild ride. *I'm on my way...and stop flirting when my boyfriend can overhear you.*

Captain Midnight swung aboard the truck bed. "Boyfriend," he grumbled to himself. "Flirting!"

He tore away the tarp covering a 50-caliber machine gun bolted to the truck bed. Releasing the tarp into the slipstream, he planted both feet firmly to ride the recoil and opened fire on the pursuing vehicles that were gaining because their drivers knew the road. The first salvo fragmented the lead truck's windshield and the men in the cab. Another sustained burst destroyed the truck's engine and that vehicle became a somersaulting, bursting ball of fire. Airborne bodies tumbled everywhere. The second driver swerved and continued pursuit.

The Gyro-Pod, nearly silent, emerged from the deeper gloom to the west at a low altitude. It hovered, then touched down on this pre-designated landing zone, a relatively flat clearing amid arid, rugged lunar-like terrain. Joyce, piloting the revolutionary craft, had been waiting nearby under cover of the night since dropping them off.

Of course, Chuck wasn't supposed to be along, not according to the original plan. Chuck had hidden away in an unused cargo compartment and waited until after they touched down to spring his surprise.

As Joyce brought the sleek aircraft to rest, its rear blades reduced in RPM's to a hushed idle. A moment later, Joyce appeared, sliding open the side hatch.

A bullet ricocheted off the 50-caliber's casing, whipping Captain Midnight's focus back to the remaining pursuit truck. Chuck started tapping his brakes as they approached the Gyro-Pod. Captain Midnight hammered out another sustained blast but the chase driver swerved again and the heavy rounds missed, kicking up a row of geysers close enough to spray the men in that truck bed with clumps of dirt. Men leaned out from either side, firing wildly. Captain Midnight again tried lining up the cab in his sights.

More bullets bounced off the 50-caliber's mount and his truck's chassis.

Then the front left tire blew. A loud *pow!* His truck veered, wobbling. Chuck shouted in angry frustration. As if in slow motion, the nose of the truck dug into the earth and started into a forward, end-over-end roll. Captain Midnight leapt clear, arcing out from the airborne truck. He heard Joyce cry out. He hit the ground with his left shoulder, allowing weight and momentum to carry him through into a somersault, coming up in a combat crouch, clutching the .45 in a two-fisted stance.

The truck had flipped over twice, coming to rest on its side. Three tires spun crazily, the fourth having torn loose and rolling off as if in a hurry to get away. Dust eddied about like a shroud. Chuck lay on his back, unmoving, some thirty paces away. Joyce came running, carrying a folded canvas stretcher, heedless of the incoming rifle fire from the truck still barreling in on them.

He faced the oncoming vehicle and started squeezing off rounds. A tight pattern of holes dotted the windshield. That truck swerved again but this time it flipped onto its side in a dirt-splashing skid that threw some men and mangled others, the sounds of grinding metal across the stony earth filling the air. He spun before that death-slide had ended.

Joyce knelt beside Chuck, checking his pulse, when he reached them. A trickle of blood seeped from Chuck's left ear. His nose was broken, bloodied. There was a peculiar, frightening caved-in look about his chest.

Joyce lifted worried eyes. "It's bad. He was thrown from the cab and the truck rolled over him. He needs medical attention *fast!*"

"Then nothing else matters. Let's get him onboard."

They placed Chuck on the stretcher, ever so gently, and rushed him to the Gyro-Pod. Joyce boarded first and together they wedged the stretcher into place.

In the near distance behind them, one of Tong's men started barking orders, establishing command, but he had to keep repeating his orders to be heard above the cries of the injured and dying. Joyce was securing the straps on Chuck when bullets started pinging off the Gyro-Pod. Captain Midnight exited the craft.

"Lift off, Joyce."

A bullet riddled the craft's bubble front. She ducked instinctively.

"But what about you? The mini-guns! We can strafe them!"

"No. This wasn't designed to be an attack craft. It's for quick insertion and retrieval only, and that's what we're using it for. Getting Chuck to medical attention is the only priority. One bullet knocks out the transmission and Chuck won't stand a chance, and neither will you."

"Aren't you coming with us?"

The incoming fire grew more concentrated. A ricochet clipped his ear lobe, drawing a droplet of blood.

"I'll provide cover fire. Now *get!* That's an order."

He rushed to the overturned truck and pried loose the 50-caliber from its mount, using the truck for cover. The Gyro-Pod lifted off. He balanced the machine gun on a fender of the truck and opened fire, swinging the mighty weapon from right to left and back again, laying down a blazing torrent of lead, thunder, and flame. Ejected brass glinted in the morning light. When the 50-caliber had chewed up its ammo belt, the abrupt absence of its hellfire was deafening. The crackle of enemy weapons and ricochets off the truck sounded like someone making popcorn. He broke open an ammo box and freed another belt for the machine gun.

The Gyro-Pod was a receding blur low in the sky, zipping away like some weird, silver-shelled insect from another world.

Suddenly, the saffron winking of rifle fire crackled from a new direction, from a jagged ridge to his left. Then something like as sledgehammer kicked him in the side of the head, and everything went black.

HE CAME to and for an instant, he was back in his bunk at the airfield in France during the War. It was time to wake up and head out on patrol over Bosch lines.

The sound of footfalls penetrated his mental fog.

His eyes snapped open and he became aware of his surroundings. He was soaked with sweat, lying flat on his back under the thatched roof of a permanent structure. Bare timber walls, the furnishings simple and rudimentary except for a pair of carbine rifles leaning together in one corner. He lay upon a pallet on the earthen floor. A bug buzzed in his ear, sounding like a dive-bomber. He had a splitting headache. And now… approaching footsteps.

He propped himself on one elbow. A hand found the reassuring butt of the .45 automatic holstered at his hip, right where it was supposed to be. By the time a head appeared through the low entrance, the pistol was extended at arm's length, safety off.

A young Chinese woman came in. She wore the coarse-textured garments of a peasant, yet there was about her an innate elegance. Almond-shaped eyes shone with intelligence. A sensuous strength curved the line of her mouth, the form of her lips. She did not bat an eye at the muzzle of the .45.

"Welcome back to the world of the living, American." She spoke a dialect he knew well.

He sighed, a drawn-out, bone-weary sound. He lowered the pistol, resting his head upon a pillow. "I may be living, but I feel more than half-dead." He spoke in Chinese. "Where am I? What day is it?"

"Wednesday. We're two kilometers from General Tong's ancestral castle. We are your friends, my husband and I."

"You're with the group that radioed the Secret Squadron?"

"Yes. General Tong is a warlord who rules this province with an iron fist, terrorizing the peasants.

Meager crops are confiscated. Those who resist are executed if caught. He levies taxes. Young girls are carried off by his "soldiers" never to be heard from or seen again. Our small group provides information to Peking but this province is so remote, there seems to be nothing our government can do. And so, Captain Midnight, we contacted you."

"When I heard that General Tong had acquired the Bellem bombsite, I had to come. And the Squadron will do what we can to help your cause. How did I get here?"

"We heard fighting and went to investigate. You were wounded in the crossfire. My husband and I brought you here."

She had a pleasant voice, but the words started to blur. Nausea overcame him. He started retching. Dry heaves. She dabbed his forehead with a damp cloth, but that didn't help. *The race for the Gyro-Pod. The blown tire, the flipping truck. Chuck on the ground. The blood snaking from his ear. His chest caved in.* Despair spread through him, his every sense yielding to uneasy, dark thoughts he'd never thought before. A corner of his rational mind told him that he was succumbing to fever, but that didn't stop the darkness borne of despair and weariness.

Chuck, at death's door. If Chuck died, the blame would fall on an egotistical fool named Albright, who'd thought himself invincible; who thought he could make a difference but who, in reality, only drew everyone he loved to their doom. Even before this, death had claimed those closest to him. Chuck's dad, Dave Ramsey. Freckle-faced, laughing Dave. The best pal, the best damn gunner, a combat flyer could have in that so-called Great War. Returning at the stroke of midnight to their base after successfully carrying out that last mission, their plane shot up, the bullet-riddled corpse of his best friend in the gunner seat...the memories haunted him still. When he returned to the States after the War, he'd visited Dave's widow. After a period of mourning, he and Pat Ramsey fell in love and married. At the time, little Chuck had resented him for marrying his mom and had blamed him for his father's death. They lost Pat when a drunken driver took her life in an accident and that's when he and Chuck finally became close, bonded in shared grief over her death. And now, he was about to lose Chuck.

What the hell good was it, even trying to make a difference? Could one man ever make a difference? Hell, no. The answer was as simple and clear-cut as that. He, James Albright—AKA the famous, fearless, indefatigable Captain Midnight—had given his all for more than two decades, could well be about to give his life...for what? Born into a troubled world of war and conflict, strife, human misery and suffering, the wicked devouring the weak. And when he died, would he leave a world any better off for his having lived? Again, hell no. He would leave a world gagging on war and greed; evil that left the good crushed and lifeless like a rose beneath a boot heel. What had been gained by a life spent trying to prevent another world war? Nothing.

Nothing had changed. Nothing ever would change. They were still developing better bombsites. They were still feeding people to the hogs.

Yes, the fever had him. He understood this even as he sank deeper into the vivid imagery of a fitful sleep. He knew he was dreaming, traveling into the past that lived within him, yet he embraced it with a mad laughter...

The air whipped their helmeted heads at terrific speed, goggled eyes squinting with wild, youthful grins into the wind, flying over the rolling farmland hills of France. Dave Ramsey divided his attention between air and ground.

Then out of the sky came the distant drone of a high-powered motor, a speck taking shape to become a bi-plane, storming at them out of the sunlight. They could not make out its markings. The other plane banked, throttle wide open, and raked them with rattling machine-gun fire.

He shoved his stick forward. They shot downward at a steep glide in pursuit of the plane that was dropping to level off with a scream of straining struts, now trying to dodge. But he and Dave were on the guy. He leveled out their bi-plane with a moaning screech and their big gun mounted on the front cowl, synchronized to shoot through the prop, yammered straight at the German plane.

But the Bosch was damn good, as so many of them were in these dogfight skies. He dodged, whipping the nose of his plane over and up, climbing, suddenly behind them, throttle and machine guns wide open.

He awoke with a start, gasping for air like a swimmer submerged underwater for too long. He sat up, eyes open, relief coursing through him at the clarity of his senses. It was night. He was alone in the hut. Wind rustled the thatched roof. The luminous dials of his watch indicated midnight. He glanced about and abruptly realized that he was not alone.

Dave Ramsey sat alongside his pallet. Dave sat cross-legged, Indian-style like a kid by a campfire. Only, somehow, it wasn't Dave; more like a shimmering, silvery presence that looked like Dave, glowing luminously but not illuminating the gloom. The spectral presence wore flight gear, the goggles pushed up onto the helmet, a bemused glint on the familiar, freckled face.

"Dave?" The name spilled unbidden from his lips in this dark little corner of reality.

The shimmering, silvery presence chuckled.

"What'sa matter, Jim? Don't you believe in ghosts?"

He sat up slowly and passed a leveled hand through the shimmer. "I guess I do now."

Another chuckle, a friendly, contagious Dave sound, carefree. But this chuckle couldn't be heard by anyone else. Something was happening here and he chose not to resist. He opened himself to the experience.

Dave said, "I know about you and Pat. Thanks for that, buddy. You took good care of her."

"I loved her, Dave. Man, it's good to see you again. I've missed you."

"And thanks for having the love and patience to raise Chuck. That means more than anything to a parent. Jim, I couldn't have done a better job myself. Chuck's becoming the man I wanted him to be and that's because of you."

"Don't thank me. Because of me, your son may have died on this mission."

"I know what happened, and I see the hell you're putting yourself through."

"And that's why you've come to see me tonight?"

Dave's spectral presence nodded, his demeanor serious. "You and me need to have a talk, old buddy."

GENERAL TONG'S lawless tyranny of the province constituted such a continuing embarrassment for Peking that the central government had willingly provided a secret staging area for this mission, complete with a field hospital.

Ikky Mudd and Tut Jones busied themselves with the Gyro-Pod, Ikky tinkering with the engine while Tut made notations on a clipboard. When Joyce approached, they paused and looked up inquisitively.

Ikky asked, "Any word on Chuck?"

"He's still in surgery. The doctors...are not optimistic."

The ground crew chief stifled a curse and turned to the pair of Nightfire fighter planes. Their bubble canopies shone in the midday sun.

"We flew these babies halfway around the world to

see some action, not to have them sit here looking pretty."

Tut always seemed unable to lose his white laboratory smock, even when on a mission. He patted the bubble-front of the Gyro-Pod.

"I came to see this invention of ours field tested. I helped design her. Now that I know what she can do, thanks to Joyce, I'd like nothing better than to see it flown back in to extract James since we do know where he is. But orders are orders."

Joyce eyed the horizon. "I should never have left him. If he dies…" The sentence trailed off.

"He won't die," said Ikky, "He's Captain Midnight. And the egghead's right. Orders are orders. Cap wanted Chuck brought here to the field hospital and that's what you did."

"But these 'friends' who are hiding him out, who radioed that he was safe and resting up but that we need to postpone recovery…can we trust them? They said the Captain would contact us. But…when?"

Ikky sighed. "Sure as shootin,' *when* is the questions of this hour."

Tut said, "They indicate some new development. I don't like it either, but I say we trust them if James does. When Captain Midnight knows what's happening, so will we."

THE BLADE of the combat knife, flung across the clearing, embedded itself in the scraggly tree, its handle quivering. Red Albright crossed the clearing and retrieved the knife.

Yuki watched him. "Your aim is true. I would not believe that you had taken a wound to the head if I had not treated you myself."

The scab at his temple was tender where the bullet had grazed him, but only a mild ache remained.

"I owe you."

They were behind the hut.

"Your reflexes are those of a warrior, ready to resume battle."

"It's just one more scar."

Her almond-shaped eyes appraised him before she spoke. "I sense something deeper within you that has been resolved. For a while, you were delirious. Then you fell into a deep sleep."

He returned the blade to its scabbard. The air was warm, although the heat of midday had begun to abate.

"You're a perceptive woman."

"Sometimes that is a blessing, sometimes a curse. Much like being a woman."

He saw no reason to tell her about his dream of Dave's visit, if indeed it had been a dream. And if it had not been a dream, what *did* happen? He was no metaphysician, but decades of world travel and adventuring had often proved to him Shakespeare's observation that there was more to heaven and earth than is dreamed of in our philosophies. He knew only that

Dave had communicated with him. And the message had been received.

Could one person make a difference?

Hell, yes. There was enough evidence of that also in the miles of blood and thunder Captain Midnight had flown through to right wrongs.

The world would never know of the momentous act of heroism performed by Dave Ramsey on the night of his death. That mission had disappeared forever into a bottomless pit marked Top Secret, but Dave's actions on that last mission turned the tide of war and saved hundreds of thousands of lives on both sides. And Chuck, at this moment seriously injured—or had he paid the ultimate price in this never-ending fight waged by the Secret Squadron to see that there would never be another "world war"? And Pat Ramsey, who until her final breath had loved her husband and their son, and a maverick flyer named Red Albright because of who these men were and how they lived their lives. He owed his best, his everything, to those people. He would *never* let them down.

What was life for if not to at least *try*, in whatever small or large measure, to leave this old world a little better off than as you found it? A human lifespan, only a grain of sand in an ocean of eternity. But let enough grains of sand activate over enough time and you had a Grand Canyon. Enough shoulders to the evolutionary wheel *could* change the world for the better. He was living the life he was born to live, and that was its purpose.

Thanks, Dave.

But this young woman did not need to hear all of that…

He heard someone approaching. He shifted a hand to the grip of his pistol, but relaxed when Zhao stepped into view.

Yuki's husband was stocky of build, wearing a frayed woolen jacket with baggy trousers. "I have news, Captain. Do you know of a scientist named von Sharpe?"

"Von Sharpe. Von Sharpe." He stayed well versed in scientific news. This, combined with a photographic memory, allowed him to extract a mental file with only two finger-snaps. "Heinrich von Sharpe. Physicist. Eccentric, some say a lunatic. Released from his professorship at Bonn after taking a swing at Albert Einstein during a symposium on the mechanics of manipulating the space-time continuum. That was two years ago. After that, von Sharpe disappeared from sight…until now, I take it."

"Dr. von Sharpe is a guest of General Tong and has been for a month. I have only just verified this."

Yuki frowned. "What would General Tong want with a physicist?"

Albright patted a pocket. "The same thing he wanted with a revolutionary bomb site. The General is setting himself up as a clearing house for weapons of the future."

Zhao nodded without enthusiasm. "The clouds of war loom always on the horizon somewhere."

"Von Sharpe is developing a new weapon and Tong is sponsoring him, or he's already developed something on his own and General Tong will put it on the black market. Either way, I've got to get my hands on whatever it is and close down the general permanently."

Yuki asked, "Is it time, then, to call in the Secret Squadron?"

Zhao said, "The man, named Mudd, was most impatient when I radioed your instructions that they stand by."

Albright chuckled. "I'll bet he was. I'll contact them in code right now. They're not going to like it, but they need to wait while Captain Midnight makes one more visit to that castle. This time, I'm taking on General Tong face to face."

He penetrated the outer defenses—over the eight-foot-high brick wall—with little difficulty, as before with Chuck, then he skirted, like the whisper of a night breeze, one of the General's roving foot patrols inside the castle grounds. He traveled as one with the night, like a wraith, to a rear wall of the main building and rappelled to a fourth-story window. The corridor was as it had been on his previous visit, chilly, stagnant, tomb-like. Stone walls. Stone floor. Dank, as if untouched by the warmth of day or by life itself.

His luck ran out when a door opened without warning and he found himself face to face with a startled young man caught in the act of buttoning his fly. The kid pawed for a shoulder-slung rifle, eyes widening in fright, and dropped to the floor, dead, seconds later but not before firing a round into the ceiling. The gunshot echoed loudly, magnified by the stone walls.

On this night, General Tong's security force had a hair-trigger response. Within five minutes he was facing the muzzles of more than a dozen rifles and pistols aimed directly at him. The .45 dropped. He raised his hands. They marched him back inside, down to the end of that fourth-floor corridor.

Before having left Yuki and Zhao, he had transmitted the Squadron's secret code, giving Ikky Mudd a specific attack time and target coordinates, cutting his numbers very close. This castle was twenty minutes away from being pulverized and there was no way to call that off. But if he wanted what the general and von Sharpe were up to, a delicate touch touch was required. Unfortunately, his touch had not been delicate enough. Not by a long shot.

A dozen sentries—hulking, bull-necked thugs—remained in the corridor while two of their number shoved him through a broad archway, into a hall of incredible dimensions, designed long ago to inspire awe. The walls were draped in exquisite Chinese dragon tapestry. One man swung shut a broad door and they took up position, arms folded, to either end of a huge table with dragons' legs. A lamp, suspended by golden chains from a vaulted ceiling so lofty it was lost in the purple shadows above, hung over the table. Smoke from a plain brass bowl upon the corner of the table writhed and penciled through the air, emitting a vague, strange perfume.

A man sat there, wearing a plain yellow robe of a hue almost identical with that of his shaved skull. His hands were large, long and bony and he held them knuckles upward, resting his chin upon their thinness. He had a great, high brow. A stern expression adorned a face dominated by narrow green eyes and a long, drooping moustache.

"I bid you welcome, Captain Midnight."

"You know who I am. You were expecting me?"

"Not tonight, I confess. But my organization has monitored your friends' radio frequency, and so I knew of the arrival of your esteemed presence." This is what a reptile would sound like if it could talk, the voice a sibilant slither, a dry tongue darting over a thin-lipped sneer. "I am General Tong. Nothing happens in this province of which I am unaware. Did you not know this, foolish American? I am most displeased. Your previous visit cost me the lives of several men."

"Looks like you've got plenty to spare."

"Had I not been," the briefest pause as if searching for the right phrase, "otherwise engaged, we would have encountered one another upon your previous visit."

"I got what I came for."

"Ah yes, the plans for the bomb site. Where are they now, might I ask?"

"They'll get to the right people."

General Tong steepled his fingers beneath his chin.

"You have a reputation for resourcefulness. Frankly, I find you exceedingly stupid. Tell me, Captain Midnight, why have you returned here to die?"

"I'm not dead yet, General."

The general leaned forward, resting a forearm on the table. "I understood from your friends' radio transmission that you also lost a man when you were here last."

"His name's Chuck Ramsey and as far as I know, he's not lost. He's still fighting even if it's on an operating table. Our kind don't give up, Tong. Chuck was… is my stepson, and he's one of the reasons I'm here. I'm not a guy to hold a grudge, but in your case, I'll make an exception. You and I have a score to settle."

General Tong arched an eyebrow. "Indeed." He indicated the closed broad door. "You have not forgotten that beyond that archway, not to mention throughout this castle, is my private army, a force sufficient to preclude any realistic thought of your escape." He indicated the thugs who remained at his side, awaiting his next order. "These two would gladly draw and quarter you before my eyes, before we roast and eat your innards. And you talk of settling scores. The bravado of the Western male has always fascinated me. And pray, what would be the second reason for your return to Castle Tong?"

"I'm here for Dr. von Sharpe. I heard he's your guest."

"Indeed." The General sat up straight. "I must confess that you are well-informed…but a trifle late. He is no longer here. You see, I was otherwise engaged during your previous visit, overseeing the feeding of Dr. von Sharpe to my hogs. They made rather quick work of him. Surely you heard."

"Then I've come for whatever he left behind."

He was talking big, sure, but he would die standing up if it came to that. In the meantime he couldn't stop calculating the odds, waiting, watching for that one opening, however slim, that Fate might provide, which he would then seize and work to death or freedom.

General Tong said, "It is only because you have no possible means of escape, Captain Midnight, that I will share with you the Professor's legacy…before you die." He reached under the table and with both hands placed upon it a strange box-like device about the size of a shoebox, the topside cylindrical with a dial, switches, a meter, antennae and assorted shiny paraphernalia. Tong smiled and spoke with pride. "This, dear sir, is a time machine."

Captain Midnight arched an eyebrow. "Indeed?" He turned and walked toward the door, not in a rush but at a leisurely pace.

Tong frowned. "Seize him!"

Captain Midnight threw shut a big bolt that securely locked the broad door from the inside. He swung around to face the pair rushing at him. Beyond them, General Tong bolted from the table, darting across the hall, cat-like, the gizmo held in both hands, toward a seemingly blank stone wall. Captain Midnight downed one of the men with a sudden death *Hiraken* blow, both fists used as club-like weapons. A bone-crushing *Empi* felled the other. Shouting and pounding came from beyond the door, but he paid no attention to that. He sprinted across the spacious hall after the general.

A section of wall magically slid upward, revealing a hidden passageway. The panel would slam shut immediately after Tong passed through it.

It was now or never.

He launched himself into a running leap and tackled Tong, taking him down just as the general and his little time machine gained the threshold.

* * *

BARE KNUCKLES rap crisply on a door.

A friendly, distracted voice responds from within. "Enter."

Chuck Ramsey briskly crosses the laboratory and places a manila folder on the corner of a table where Red Albright and Tut Jones stand, examining a strange-looking gadget about the size of a shoebox, unlike anything Chuck has ever seen before. Arizona sunshine pours through a row of windows.

"Red, here's the update you wanted on that mission to China, the General Tong affair."

"Thanks, Chuck."

Albright and Tut are engrossed in the strange gizmo.

Chuck has something pressing on his mind. Professional cool cracks beneath impetuous yearning.

"Uh, Cap, this trip you're taking to China…uh, can I go with you?"

Albright looks up with the smallest of smiles.

"That's been taken care of, Chuck." He indicates the folder. "File that under Case Closed."

Disappointment, and nothing but.

"You mean…we're not, I mean, you're not going to China?"

Captain Midnight sends Tut a wink, unseen by Chuck, before they return their attention to the gizmo.

"That's right, Chuck. General Tong's time ran out."

V

LAST STAND: A WESTERN
SHORT STORY

LAST STAND

THEY HELD THE HIGH GROUND.

Below a natural citadel, formed by a ring of boulders, a steep drop-off of several hundred feet made for an eminently defensible position. The outcrop of boulders was flanked to the rear by a rocky incline, a clearing of murky shadows before a stand of conifers.

Blaze crouched, his Winchester at the ready, scanning through a narrow break between the boulders, what he could see of the moon-washed base of this towering rock formation. He discerned no movement down there.

A gentle breeze sighed through the pines. There was a muted crackle of insects and somewhere nearby an owl hooted. Otherwise, there was only the stillness of night beneath a quarter moon and an infinity of winking stars.

A few braves had tried to scale the rock citadel

during the fierce daylight fighting. Their bodies were sprawled across jagged rocks below.

"What time is it?" asked Kate.

She knelt on one knee beside Blaze, behind an adjacent boulder, her eyes and her Winchester scanning the uphill clearing.

He could have brought out his watch and read the time easily by the moonlight, but a glance at the moon's position was enough.

"It's three o'clock, or just after."

She sighed with exhaustion, apprehension, and defeat. "I can't remember the last time I slept, but I don't feel tired at all."

"That's nature's way of giving you a fighting chance," said Blaze. "It's because we're surrounded by hostiles who want to kill us."

She was a few years younger than her husband. Kate had intelligent brown eyes that highlighted a face of high cheekbones and saucy, full lips. Her shoulder-length chestnut hair was tied back beneath a flat-brimmed black hat. She wore a man's blue work shirt, a leather vest, a denim skirt with a silver conch belt around her trim waist, and riding boots.

"Nothing's happened since sunset," she noted. "It's so quiet, J.D. Do you think they're out there?"

Blaze was dark-haired and well muscled. A big man, he wore a weathered wide-brimmed hat, a lightweight pullover shirt with a neckerchief, Levi's and well-worn boots. A holstered Remington .44-40 revolver was on his left hip, butt forward for quick cross-draw. A cap box holding his cartridges was on his right hip. Criss-crossed bandoleers held ammunition for the rifles.

"They're out there," he said. "These fellas don't give up. They just don't cotton to doing things at night."

J.D. and Kate Blaze were the only husband and wife team of gunfighters-for-hire that Blaze had ever heard tell of. If you hired Blaze, who had earned a reputation across the states and territories as a man more than fast and capable with any sort of gun, you also got peppery Kate in the bargain. They'd had a justice of the peace marry them two days after they met in El Paso, and that was five years ago. Ever since, they'd worked as a team from Canada to Mexico, from San Francisco to Omaha, hiring out their gun skills to ranchers, the railroad, bank syndicates, anyone in need of the best shootists for hire—who just happened to be husband and wife—*if* the client was willing to meet their price. They never rode the outlaw trail. They had never spent a night apart.

It had been an eventful five years. They had seen and fought their way through practically every situation imaginable...*except* being surrounded by Indians, vastly outnumbered. The Indians bid their time in the dark of night, patiently awaiting the first light of dawn when they would overrun and slaughter this man and woman crouched together behind the boulders.

The ambush had been well staged. Blaze and Kate were pulling up out of an arroyo, which they'd had to traverse, when gunfire opened up on them from rock formations on both sides. Their horses had been shot out from under them. The braves had emerged then, ferocious apparitions wearing bandoleers of ammunition and everything from Civil War ex-military garb to breechcloths, bandanas wrapped about their heads, wearing knee-high moccasins, armed with knives and rifles. But before they could close in, the Blazes had grabbed the saddlebags with their money and managed to scurry up the steep rocks to this defensible position. In the light that remained the Blazes stood off wave after wave of attacking hostiles.

But Blaze didn't kid himself. It was luck alone that had spared them thus far.

Bullets had whistled and ricocheted from below and from the trees across the clearing behind them. A flying chip of rock left a razor-thin slash across Blaze's left cheekbone, but the droplets of blood had congealed and that was the only wound sustained thus far.

"Well," said Kate, "we gave it our best shot and we almost made it. How far is it to the border?"

"About fifteen miles to Naco," he said. "And one of us can still make it."

They'd been on their way to Mexico with ten thousand dollars stuffed in their saddlebags.

"What do you mean, *one* of us can still make it?"

"It's a few hours until dawn," he estimated. "That's when they'll attack."

"We could slip past them on foot in the dark," she offered. "It could be done."

"Maybe, but that's not what I have in mind. As soon as they overrun this position and find us both gone, they'll track us down easy. They'll be on horseback, and we'll be on foot. They'd kill us and take our money."

She frowned. "You said one of us could make it."

"Uh huh. I think I can get us out of here. I'll lead you to the river." He handed her the saddlebags. "You take these. When we get to the river, we'll split up. Follow the river south. I'll come back up here and hold them off, and give you a chance to get away. I'll catch up with you in Mexico."

Her frown deepened. "What the hell are you talking about, Blaze?"

"Just follow the San Pedro," he said. "It will take you into Mexico, and there you can buy transportation first class to anywhere."

"If I got there before you," she said, "I'd wait, thanks. But just out of curiosity, what about you, after I've merrily traipsed off with our life savings over my shoulder? What will you do?"

"I told you. I'll slip back and be right here when dawn breaks like they expect. Don't you see? If we're both gone, they'll track us down and we're both dead. I've got enough ammunition to thin their ranks and make the survivors want to be someplace else. Then I'll catch up with you and we'll live happily ever after."

She shook her head. "I don't know, J.D. Right now, braves from their village are on their way here to be part of this and avenge those we killed."

"What does that have to do with anything?" he said gruffly.

She studied him in the moonlight. "You're a gallant

man, did you know that?" She sighed again. "Very well. I'll be an obedient wife. Your way does make sense."

He blinked. He hadn't expected convincing her would be quite so easy.

"Uh, all right then. I reckon we'd better head out."

"There is one thing before we go."

He paused. "What's that?"

"Well, first off, are you sure these people who want to kill us won't attack us during the hours of darkness like you said?"

"I reckon I'm as sure about that as I am about anything,"

"Good," she whispered huskily. "Because, J.D., I'm sorry as hell but all of this insanity, this violence and bloodshed and us maybe about to die...J.D., I need something to make me feel *alive* before we say good-bye. Do you understand?" She chuckled. There was a trace of lewdness to the pleasant, softly rippling sound. "Big man, I'm not saying goodbye until I get some of what I like best about you."

Blaze said, "Huh?"

"Darling," said Kate, her whisper breathy in the closeness between them, "it's your turn to be an obedient husband and give me what I *need.*"

Well the hell, thought Blaze. It seemed only right that their last goodbye *should* be their best.

And so, there on the ground, beneath the cover of the boulders in the stillness of the night, he drew her to him and drew her lips to his. Their kiss pulsated, her tongue slithering in and out of his mouth, hot and wet.

He eased his free hand up to caress her breasts, cupping first one and then the other the way she liked, his thumb lightly brushing alternately across her nipples. When the kiss broke, she arched back her head with a sigh, revealing the curve of her throat. He lowered his lips to her throat. She moaned when he kissed her there, the fingers of one of her hands drifting across his chest and abdomen, lower to close around his hardening shaft. She stroked him through the Levi's, a loose-fisted, sensuous up down jerking motion. Their lips clenched again, fiery. His hands slid down her waist to her rump. He grabbed hold of its firmness, yanking her up to him. Their loins met through the material of their clothing, and they began a primal grinding.

Kate gasped. "Take me, baby! Here! *Now!*"

"My pleasure," said Blaze.

The heated immediacy of the moment made the world beyond them, and the danger in it, vanish in a surge of the lust that had sparked them since the day they met.

Easing a hand up each of her smooth thighs, he lifted the hem of her skirt to around her waist and lowered her undergarments. Her legs were bent at the knee, slightly spread. She undid his Levi's and brought them down to mid-thigh. She guided him into her, and they each emitted a drawn-out groan. His callused hands tightened on her smooth, naked bottom and their hip-thrusts met, hard and fast. Kate crossed her ankles behind Blaze's driving hips. Her head whipped back and forth, her chestnut hair splayed out upon the ground, eyes clamped shut, her mouth open and twisting with silent moans. Her fists hammered his back.

She came again and again.

When her spasmodic bucking subsided, Blaze eased up on his pace but did not stop. His hips rolled from side to side, and before long her pelvis was jerking again, uncontrollably.

"Oh! Oh my goodness, honey." She gasped close to his ear. "You're making it happen *again"*

This time he let himself release and their bodies quaked together, as one.

WITH THE COMING of dawn gray light slowly revealed the valley beyond the base of the boulders.

Blaze viewed the scene along the length of his Winchester, which rested in a notch between two boulders overlooking the drop-off. The high vantage point provided him with a wide field of vision.

The course of the river in the distance was marked by a wending line of cottonwoods, their bright green a striking contrast to the drab flatness of the landscape beyond this southernmost tip of the Mule Mountains. Arid, wide-open prairie stretched south to mountains that shimmered in the distance, in Mexico

The air retained the nip of night, which would not

dissipate, Blaze knew, until the rising sun crested the mountains behind him.

By that time, he expected to be dead.

He hoped Kate believed his rosy picture of a reunion. But she was right about the hostiles bringing in more braves during the night. And so, after their lovemaking, they had gathered themselves and Blaze led the way from this position, cautiously, through the night.

They froze in their tracks, at one point, for a full five minutes. Indians had passed within fifteen feet of their place of concealment. Then they continued on and eventually reached the banks of the river that flowed placidly beneath the cottonwoods, sparkling in the moonlight like diamonds on black glass.

After a prolonged embrace, after kisses and vows of endearment, and Kate's tears, she left, walking stoically away, along the river heading south. She would reach Naco by midday, sooner if she found a horse. He could see her yet in his mind's eye, his last view of her before she rounded a bend in the river and disappeared from his sight.

Her Winchester was over one shoulder and, over the other rested the saddlebags that held five years of their savings, the result of severe budgeting by Kate as they'd traveled, working jobs, getting paid. She kept the books. They'd finished their last job, safeguarding a shipment for a mining company out of Silver City a week earlier. It was said that gunslingers never died of old age. It was their intention to prove themselves the exception to that rule, to peacefully live out the rest of their days as gringo ranchers, far from the sound of gunfire. But there had been no way to reach the border without crossing Indian land...

Watching her go, Blaze had tried to ignore the lump in his throat, the empty feeling in his heart.

He'd retraced his route back to this position, encountering two separate groups of hostiles during the return trip, but remained undetected. They were indeed beefing up for a full-scale assault. As he worked his way back, he rethought his decision and the reasons for making it, time and again with his every stealthy step. But he could think of no alternative, considering that his only priority was to see Kate removed from harm's way.

So now here he was, back amid his citadel of boulders, his ammunition dwindled, the enemy reinforced, poised to attack.

A single rifle shot cracked, flat and clear from below, a signal that heralded a barrage of fire from below and from the trees across the clearing.

He fired through the notch between the boulders, levered another round into the Winchester's chamber and sent that one down where the base of his citadel remained shrouded in the half-light of predawn. He saw no one, and so fired at the saffron muzzle flashes of their rifle fire.

Rounds ricocheted off boulders and geysered up clumps of earth close to where he flattened himself to the ground making a minimal target. At the base of the drop-off, braves were scaling the rocks, starting up at him.

The hairs at the back of his neck curled, and he rolled over onto his back, swinging the Winchester around in time to spot a pair of braves advancing across the clearing. They saw him roll over and opened fire. He returned fire and saw one drop. He lever-actioned another round.

His right arm suddenly felt as if slammed by a hammer and stabbed with a hot poker at the same time, and even as the shot from his rifle dropped the second Indian in the clearing, he knew he'd been hit.

He tried to chamber another round. But he was right-handed, and his right hand would not respond. Warm moistness started to soak his shirt around the wound. He could tell that the bullet had passed clean through, high on the right. The pain would come, but right now he felt only a hammering numbness there.

Two more braves popped up onto the boulders, having scaled up. They saw him sprawled there with his useless rifle and wounded right arm. They emitted blood-curdling cries, drew wide-bladed knives, and crouched to spring on him.

Blaze summoned strength from his left arm and used it to fling the rifle at the closest brave, the rifle stock striking right where he aimed it, in the Indian's crotch. The warrior grunted and folded, then lost his balance and disappeared from sight over the edge of the boulder. His body could be heard hitting the rocks.

A rifle shot sounded from behind Blaze.

A bullet blew away the top of the second Indian's head.

Gunfire continued from the trees, across the clearing. And, of course, more braves would soon be scaling the rocks. Bullets whizzed everywhere.

He scuttled, crab-like, across the ground toward the inky shadow of a mesquite tree where low branches would provide some concealment. As he moved, he twisted his left hand and drew his revolver. The .44-40 would be good for close-in fighting, and that would come soon enough. Halfway to the tree, he saw two more braves start across the clearing, well beyond the accurate range of his pistol.

Another rifle shot from nearby.

One of the braves was kicked off his feet as if punched by an invisible giant fist. The second turned to retreat but was dropped by another rifle shot.

Blaze gained the mesquite tree at the same time as Kate.

A chinstrap held her flat-brimmed hat behind her chestnut hair. Her brown eyes burned like embers. Smoke curled from the barrel of her Winchester.

Blaze said, "Well hello, darlin'."

There was an abrupt lull in the gunfire and war-whooping from below and from across the clearing.

Kate started to embrace him, then saw his wound. "You've been hit!" She rushed to examine his wound, muttering an unladylike curse.

He said, "I don't know why I'm not surprised to see you."

"You didn't think for a minute that I'd run out on you, did you?" she snapped tartly. "If I'd said I was coming back, you would have made trouble. The main thing was to get our money out of here. We don't want these sons of bitches to get their hands on it. By the way, we've got to stop this bleeding." She tore at her shirt and used the material to stuff into his wound. This did elicit a wince of pain before the throbbing numbness resumed. "There," she said. "You won't die from that."

Blaze couldn't help himself. He grinned. "You always were the pragmatic one."

Kate rewarded the grin with a kiss to his lips. The kiss was moist, pliant, fleeting.

"That money is waiting for us," she said. "I hid it along the river. Only I know where. I had to come back, J.D. I figured I could outflank them and pick off a few in the process like I did."

Blaze held her cleft, Nebraska farm girl chin between the thumb and index finger of his good hand, and looked straight into those brown eyes that had always bewitched him,

"We're not going to make it," he said. "I wish you hadn't come back. I really do. You're my main concern, not the money. They're regrouping. They've got us surrounded and they're fixing to overrun us any minute now in one massed attack, and that will be the end of it."

A morning dove cooed.

Or maybe it was a signal.

Her eyes shone with strength and determination. "Blaze, *if we* get out of this, we get out together. If it ends here, we go out standing together."

A single rifle shot cracked in the crisp morning air. Before it could echo away, gunfire and war cries resumed, this time from every direction. The air became thick with flying bullets.

Blaze grunted. "Damned if I *won't* stand."

He struggled to his feet, realizing how he'd been weakened by his loss of blood. Kate helped him gain his footing. He retained his hold on the revolver.

She turned her back to his. She levered a fresh round into her Winchester.

"I love you, J.D."

"I'm damn proud to be the man you love," Blaze heard himself say. He thought, *I never talk like that!* Even the hammering numbness of his shoulder was forgotten. "I love you, Katie. I'll see you on the other side."

They were closing in from the trees now, springing over boulders, nearly a dozen of them having scaled the rocks, attacking from every direction.

Blaze and Kate stood back to back and met the assault with their weapons blazing.

VI

EAGLE PARK SLIM

EAGLE PARK SLIM

IT STARTED SNOWING ON THE DRIVE UP TO THE GIG. BY five o'clock in the afternoon the day had already turned dark. Flurries swirled in the headlights of the band van as we left the rainy streets of Denver, bound for a ski resort in the mountains.

Four of us rode in that Econoline van. Jeff, the acerbic longhair transplant from Baltimore. Dynamite drummer. And Mouse. Dapper, small-boned blond guy. Impish. Laidback, the way most bass players are. Me. The harp player. In the blues, the harmonica is a harp. The Mississippi saxophone. I hailed from the Midwest, a recent transplant. Everyone in Denver in those days was from somewhere else.

And there was Slim.

We were Eagle Park Slim & The Mile Hi Blues Band.

Slim (I never knew his real name) was a guitar player spawned by the rough and tumble, take no prisoners world of the St. Louis blues scene which at that time—the mid-1970s--was a musical school of hard knocks ruled by giants like Albert King and Chuck Berry and Ike and Tina Turner. In fact, a Slim claim to fame was that he had once worked in a band with Chuck Berry's piano man, Johnnie Johnson, as well as a sideman for some of the more famous blues and R&B stars who passed through St. Louis, accompanied on one-nighters by pickup musicians like Slim provided by the local promoter.

Slim never did make it big. He only ever laid down a handful of obscure recordings that few people ever heard, or heard of. Eventually he quit St. Louis and moved west where he'd set up shop fronting a band in Denver for about ten years.

Eagle Park Slim was a black man of a light chocolate hue, in his mid-thirties. Average in height and build. He carried himself quietly with his head always held high. Not a flashy dresser but well turned out, and never without aviator shades and headband. Soft-spoken, he emanated an earthy dignity. A troubadour. A man of the people . . . though so focused on his own goals, his perceptions, his energy, that he seldom expressed much interest in the mundane affairs of everyday life going on around him.

Women found him irresistible.

And nothing, I mean nothing, slowed Slim down. Twenty minutes before the gig and a band member calls in sick? No problem. A band member can't be found? Not to worry. As Slim often said, one monkey don't stop no show. He would get on the phone and by starting time he would kick off the night with his first hot guitar lick and the house would be rocking to a full band as scheduled. The Mile Hi Blues Band worked three-four nights a week at the rock clubs in Denver and at the ski resorts and hippie bars in the mountains like the gig we were traveling to tonight along a blacktop two-lane that curved and climbed, becoming steeper by the mile.

Jeff was driving. A cigarette dangled from the corner of his mouth. He was cursing up a blue streak, using his left palm to wipe clear the steamed-up windshield while driving with his right, muttering, "Why the fuck does the weather turn shitty every time I have to drive?"

Mouse fired up a joint.

"Just a cowinky-dink," he said with a stoner smile. "Roll with it, man."

Mouse and I rode in the back seat. Slim, as usual, rode shotgun next to whoever was driving. Our equipment, drums and amplifiers etc., were packed in behind us in the van's cargo area.

Mouse passed me the joint.

I took a toke and said nothing. I'd seen the weather forecast before the guys picked me up. Heavy snows were expected. It was February in Colorado.

Slim didn't smoke pot, at least not in front of any of us, and he didn't like whoever was driving to get high either, which also contributed to Jeff's irritability.

Slim said, "Shoot, snow don't bother me none. I'm

from St. Louis, man." He was addressing us in general, speaking to no one in particular. "It snowed like all get-out the night I backed Jimmy Reed. I ever tell you fellas about that?"

My ears perked up. Jimmy Reed was a famous blues singer. By the time Slim encountered him, Jimmy Reed would have been on the tail end of a long career of radio and jukebox hits delivered in a slurred, down-home style that had been big with both white and black audiences. His songs like *Big Boss Man, Baby What You Want Me to Do?* and *Bright Lights, Big City* were recorded by everyone from Elvis to the Rolling Stones. It was widely known that his famous slurred delivery was the result of too much whiskey and too much dope.

Slim was saying, "Whoweee, that night was a mess and yeah, man, it was snowing big time. Jimmy Reed was supposed to go on at 9 o'clock. I had my boys set up at the club at 7:30. I was on guitar and had me a cat on drums and a boy what played bass. The record covers always show Jimmy playing a guitar but they told us he'd only be strumming some and I'd be handling most of the guitar work. That was okay with me.

"So we're sitting around, me and the fellas, shooting the breeze. Folks showing up for the show even with the snow and all. Jimmy Reed, he could always draw a crowd. The tables were filling up. But no Jimmy Reed. Then about 8:45, a taxi drops the cat off and the driver comes in demanding his fare and he ain't cool about it because Jimmy had puked and passed out in his cab. And Jimmy Reed? He's raggedy as hell, man. His shirt was buttoned wrong. He smelled like a distillery. And he didn't have no guitar! That's right, the boy was drunk as a skunk and he wasn't carrying no axe. Man, it was sure 'nuff a stone mess."

Slim was still going strong, uninterrupted, when we left the highway to commence the final steep climb up to the ski area. Not that the monologue was bothering anyone. Jeff was busy with his driving, peering through the windshield at the snow that was only intensifying in our headlights. Mouse and I stayed busy with another joint. The four of us had been working together for more than a year. We knew and were tolerant of each other.

I've known other creative people--musicians, actors, writers--who had a similar personality trait as Slim. Loved to tell you about themselves. And it was Slim's band, after all. No one among us would ever think of trying to dissuade the man from going on about himself. We were three young white-boy musicians learning "the blues life" from one who'd been born into it. Slim rarely repeated his stories and most of them were damn interesting with the ring of truth.

He was saying, "So the owner of the place, who booked the gig, he's on my case to sober Jimmy up. Well now, we are already running late with a full house. Getting that man sober wasn't so easy. My bass man and the drummer, they was scrambling around trying to find a guitar for him to play. Me, I'm getting Jimmy sobered up with all the coffee I can make him drink. And Jimmy, he don't like being sober.

"I get him to the men's room and fix up his appearance best I can and you know what? While we're alone, he tells me to step back and check him out. Can I tell if he's peed in his pants? Lord have mercy! That's what he said. What's it called when that happens? See, he couldn't always hold it when he was drinking hard like he always was. Told me he wore dark slacks so people wouldn't notice. Well man, I was embarrassed but he looked okay to me and I told him so but y'know I'm thinking, Lord have mercy, this boy's in almost as bad shape as Little Willie John, who they had us backing up the month before.

"Little Willie John, he was higher than a Georgia pine but he was a sissy boy on top of that, prancing all over the place like a girl and actin' the fool. Jimmy Reed, he liked the women right enough, far as I could tell, but he was a damn handful and no mistake. Anyway, come 9:30 and I had the boy on stage, halfway sober, and my fellas had finally found him a guitar."

As Slim got to this part of his story, our Econoline van, which by that time must have been looking like a misshapen snowball on wheels, was drawing up before the chalet-style resort. The white stuff was really coming down. Not a wind-blown blizzard but one of those heavy, steady, silent snow. Skiers had booked rooms for the night and were already well-lubed, ecstatic about the heavy snowfall. It promised to be a great day on the slopes tomorrow. As for tonight, the band had arrived and the party was on!

It was a crowd of squeaky clean white professionals; mostly thirty-somethings. Upwardly Mobile Young Professionals, they were calling them in those days. Yuppies. A well-healed, vibrant bunch, their amped-up behavior fueled by alcohol and hormones.

We unloaded our gear in record time. Within minutes Slim kicked off the first number, an up-tempo shuffle. We were a tough, tight, rockin' little blues band with our bad-to-the-bone rhythm section—Jeff's propulsive drumming over Mouse's smooth bass, walking the blues like nobody's business--and my amplified blues harp lines weaving in and out of Slim's vocals and blues-drenched guitar playing. We packed that dance floor in no time.

And yet for me, the set seemed lacking. While he sang his blues and the up-tempo boogie-rock numbers without missing a beat, Slim's eyes never stopped gazing over the bobbing heads of his audience to the windows beyond them beyond which the snow fell.

When we took our break between the two 45-minute sets we'd been hired to play, Slim ordered a rum and coke at the bar, his usual drink on a gig, and eased off into a corner where he sat alone on a bar stool, a figure of isolation, contemplating the snow accumulation.

Jeff and Mouse were doing their best to score female companionship but with no luck far as I could see.

Me? I had a wife back in Denver. I nursed a beer and stayed to myself. Truth is, that snow coming down and the knowledge that we were on top of a mountain and were going to have to drive back down after the gig had me sort of preoccupied.

I elbowed my way through the crowd and joined Slim in his relative isolation. Referring to the weather outside, I said, "Sure is coming down."

He nodded, saying nothing.

I said, "Slim, you okay?"

The response was a mild shrug. No change in his stoic expression. Nothing to say, We watched the snowfall for a while in silence.

Then I said, "I'm not looking forward to driving back in that shit either, but it'll be okay. One more set and we're gone." I took the liberty of nudging him in the ribs with an elbow. I said, with a nod at the weather, "This monkey ain't stopping no show."

Slim did not respond.

During his second set, Eagle Park Slim sang and played and we accompanied him and the drunken yuppies in their expensive ski duds had themselves a natural ball. But Slim did not grace them with the amusing, rhyming patter he sometimes delivered between songs when the spirit was on him. We rushed through the last few songs. No one on the dance floor noticed and no one in the band cared. After the last number me, Mouse and Jeff went about breaking down the equipment in record time.

A lucky break was that Slim didn't have to track

down the money. He was sought out and handed a check while we were loading the van. Waiting to get paid after a band job can be a time-consuming drag, but I guess they appreciated that four hired hands who weren't spending the night just wanted to start home.

We brushed snow off the windshield and side windows of the van. No one was saying a word when we left the parking lot with Jeff again resuming his duty at the wheel. There was a shared relief at being underway. But the drive down off the mountain was going to be dangerous and everyone knew it.

The resort's private road was narrow and had been plowed, but the snow kept coming down so fast, we were only able to stay on it thanks to the fencing that ran along its either side. There was no other traffic coming down. Taillights to follow would have been nice. The only sound in our van was that of the wind-shield wipers laboring to keep the windshield mostly clear. We literally inched our way along. Vehicles passed us going up slow in the opposite direction. There was a sheer drop-off on the far side of that lane.

We rode in silence. Collective tension is a palpable thing. Jeff muttered a curse every minute or so when our tires would lose traction. The van would go into a short skid before he regained control. Mouse produced a joint. He took a long hit and offered it to me. I declined. My gut was in a knot of apprehension. I could barely breathe. Directly in front of me in the passenger seat, Slim sat erect with his back straight and his head high.

Our van's headlights picked up a young woman riding on the hood of a car as it crept its way uphill. She was fully dressed with her legs stretched out before her, bracing herself on the hood, leaning back against the passenger-side windshield. She wore no jacket or any protection against the heavy snow. She was laughing, having the time of her life.

Jeff said under his breath, "Acid tripper."

I said, "You're doing fine, Jeff. Seems like the snow is lightning up."

Mouse took another hit on his joint. The van was filling with smoke but, being pot smoke, it wasn't that bad.

Slim said nothing.

Around another curve, a man in a parka stood in our path, waving us down by broadly semaphoring both arms over his head. There's a saying, "he wore a deer in the headlights look." That was this guy.

Jeff started pumping the brakes. Our van slowed and began to swerve. I know I wasn't the only one holding my breath. We could have easily skidded into those vehicles in the oncoming lane. Or we could've crossed into that lane and gone over the ledge of the drop-off. Or we could have killed the man waving us down. Hell, we could've done all three.

We glided to a halt with the van's front end stopped inches short of him.

The man seemed unfazed by that but he had not lost the wild look in his eyes. He was now waving to indicate the drop-off.

"I just went over! Oh shit, man! My new car . . . I just went over! My car . . . It fell over that cliff and I just now climbed back up. Oh, shit!"

Slim broke his silence.

"Anyone hurt?"

"No! I'm alone. But it's my new skis! My new skis are down there!"

Jeff said, "Get in. We'll take you to a phone."

"I can't do that," the guy babbled. "I've already paid for my room at the lodge. My car! My skis!"

And with that he flung himself frantically away and went about trying to flag down the next approaching vehicle heading uphill.

Jeff rolled up his window. We continued on. No one spoke.

I had not believed my own words when I'd commented on the snow abating. It is my nature to think positive even when it looks like I'm about to die in a snow storm on a remote Rocky Mountain road. But within another half-mile or so, the flurries did diminish noticeably in our headlights. And lo and behold, by the time the resort's access road rejoined the state highway, miracle of miracles, the flurries were gradually becoming nothing more than a cold gentle mist!

In Colorado when it comes to snow, elevation can be everything. Snow above a specified elevation with rain at the lower elevations is a staple of the winter weather forecast.

Jeff rolled his window down a crack, shook a

cigarette loose from his pack, stuck one in the corner of his mouth and fired it with the dash lighter.

I said, "Good driving, Jeff."

Jeff mumbled through a haze of cigarette smoke, "What the fuck was I supposed to do? We made it."

He dialed in Denver's FM jazz station on the dash radio, tuned low.

Mouse said, "Hey man, pull over when you see a liquor store. I need a can of beer after that ride."

I said, "Sounds good. Make that a six-pack and I'm in."

And Slim said, "So I help Jimmy on with his guitar and what happens? The boy gets all tangled up in the doggone strap. And all I could say to myself was, Lord have mercy, this is going to be a long night."

A LOOK AT NIGHT WIND

BY STEPHEN MERTZ

Robin Curtis and her son Paul have come to Devil Creek to start over after her bitter divorce. Also new to the area is Mike Landware, a writer haunted by the death of his wife. Neither of them is looking for love or trouble, but in Devil Creek, it's possible they'll find both.

At first Devil Creek seems like an idyllic small town, but it's not long until things begin to go horribly wrong. A young hoodlum takes an automatic weapon into town for a killing spree that shocks everyone. The same night, a serial killer begins stalking the women of the community. When Paul goes missing in the mountains, it's up to Robin and Mike to find him and to find out what's going on in their new home . . . before it's too late and another victim is added to the growing death toll.

AVAILABLE FROM STEPHEN MERTZ AND WOLF-PACK PUBLISHING

ALSO BY STEPHEN MERTZ

Night Wind

Devil Creek

Blood Red Sun

Devil Creek

The Korean Intercept

The Castro Directive

Hank & Muddy

Cold In The Grave

The Moses Deception

ABOUT THE AUTHOR

Stephen Mertz is an American fiction author who is best known for his mainstream thrillers and novels of suspense. His work covers a wide variety of styles from paranormal dark suspense (*Night Wind* and *Devil Creek*) to historical speculative thrillers (*Blood Red Sun*) and hardboiled noir (*Fade to Tomorrow*). Mertz is also a popular lecturer on the craft of writing and has appeared as a guest speaker before writer's groups and at universities.

Steve's writing output increased dramatically when he emerged as one of the country's most in-demand writers of adventure paperback novels, averaging four books per year for ten years. His work on Don Pendleton's Mack Bolan series is regarded by fans as some of the best in that series. He also created the Mark Stone: MIA Hunter and Cody's Army series, written under the pseudonyms Jack Buchanan and Jim Case respectively.

Stephen Mertz lives in the American Southwest, and he is always at work on a new book.

Find Stephen online:
www.stephenmertz.com

www.ingramcontent.com/pod-product-compliance
Lightning Source LLC
Chambersburg PA
CBHW020912180626
46816CB00007BA/2360